HIDING in
plain sight

PALMETTO
P U B L I S H I N G
Charleston, SC
www.PalmettoPublishing.com

Hardcover ISBN: 979-8-8229-4523-4
Paperback ISBN: 979-8-8229-4057-4
eBook ISBN: 979-8-8229-4058-1

HIDING in
plain sight

Brian Brady

DEDICATION

To all the San Franciscans who love their City by the Bay,
their Giants, 49ers, Warriors, and Sharks. Who, when asked
where they grew up, answer first with their high school – no
matter where they may have gone to college - then their parish, or neighborhood. And who still treasure having grown
up in the greatest city in the world. To the SFPD who police
this great city. And always, to Gerry.

ACKNOWLEDGEMENTS

It is always difficult to try and single out individuals for their contributions when there are so many who have contributed. Sometimes it's a story or an anecdote, and often it's just a simple memory, or even a single line that allows for some creative embellishment. In this story I want to acknowledge 'George,' the bartender at Original Joe's, Westlake. He's real… and he's a great bartender and an old friend.

I have to acknowledge a firefighter friend from my time in the LA area, Bob Cavaglieri, who, after reading my first book, told me there weren't enough Italians or firefighters in the story. This is for you Bob — Italians, firefighters, and a surprise. Jim and Laurie Kehl, old friends who contributed a single line that developed into a complete chapter. And finally, Westlake Joe's, technically Original Joe's, Westlake — a tradition, a landmark, and a place that everyone, in and around San Francisco, knows and loves. Michael Connelly has Musso & Frank's, and I've got Westlake Joe's!

TABLE OF CONTENTS

CHAPTER 1

The cinder blocks have been flaking away far longer than anyone can recall or even care. Small piles of white-gray dust lie on the ground around the perimeter of the little building. He doesn't care. It is ideal.

He found it entirely by accident right after he arrived in town a couple of months before. He has been traveling for weeks and needs a place to call home base while he scouts the area.

He's been driving around, trying to find an address posted in an ad for an entirely different property, when he sees the 'For Rent or Lease' sign hanging on the chain link fence. The sign is old, the building is even older. But it looks perfect, located as it is, in an industrial neighborhood in the Potrero Hill area, on the east side of town, not far from the piers on the bay. Mission Bay and Potrero Hill had been gentrified, a fancy word for trendy and expensive, but this area, called Dogpatch, is still cheap.

After he calls the number on the sign, Mr. Osborne, the owner of the place, comes to show it to him. It is a standalone building with two large garage doors, a parking area, and a small living area in the rear.

"My old man had a towing business," Osborne explains. "I worked for him for a while, after school and over summers. He used this lot here to store cars and then used those two bays in the front building to do some minor repairs. He even set up this apartment in the back, and lived there for a while when he was younger. San Francisco rents were high even back then. Then he met my mother, and she didn't want anything to do with living in a garage."

Talkative old guy, Osborne… "I even lived here for a while myself, after I moved out of my folks' place. But when I met my wife, may she rest in peace, she didn't want to live here, either. I guess women are funny that way."

"Yeah, I suppose they are," he replies with a slight smile, hoping that would help move Osborne to the possibility of a moment of silence.

"Anyway," Osborne continued, unfazed, "with all the homeless people showing up in the city, I've been kind of worried about this place. I want to have it occupied. So, what do you think?"

He looks around. This location on Illinois Street is isolated and private. The two bays would easily accommodate his two vans, and the chain link fence around the property speaks for itself: 'Keep Out.'

"I think it'll be a good home base for me and my business," he says.

"Oh? What kind of business are you in?"

"I'm starting a painting business. I've got a couple of jobs lined up so far, and if they go well I may even add an employee."

They agree on a price, and he counts out three months' rent, in cash, into Osborne's gnarled hands.

He moves in that night, experiencing that feeling, a combination of nervous anticipation and excitement, almost tingly. He gets that feeling every time he moves into a new place, wondering just who and what the area has to offer.

Now he is looking forward to something new, while making sure he doesn't leave any evidence behind. The neighborhood is perfect, virtually empty at night, and occupied daily by blue-collar workers coming in for their day jobs. No clubs or bars means no nighttime foot traffic. There are a couple of restaurants that cater to the breakfast, lunch, and maybe an early dinner or beer crowd, then on the road home. It is buttoned up by 8:00pm.

CHAPTER 2

The sweat dripping down his back could be the heat of the afternoon sun beating down on his coveralls, but it could just as easily have been the excitement and anticipation coursing through his veins. He stands next to the open door of his van, tipping up a bottle of water, taking a few swallows. While he drinks, he surreptitiously glances around. It won't be long now.

He put the water down inside the van and slides the door partly closed, revealing more of the logo on the side – the words Harris Painting, with a loose, dripping swash of paint underlining 'Harris'. Walking back toward the church, he can see a few of the kids getting out of school now. He looked down at his watch. 2:30. Right on time.

He can't believe his good luck, landing a cash painting job at a church… if they only knew. Then to top it off, there's a school next door with a bevy of young girls for his perusal. He always loved young girls, but his attraction to these young girls had also cost him dearly. Never again, he is smarter and much better organized today. Now he waits for his favorite.

He moves toward the front door so he can stand behind one of the pillars and watch the girls as they streamed away from the school. Particularly the older ones. Some of the older girls, just on the threshold of adulthood, still had no idea of the effect of those plaid skirts that revealed their pretty legs. He sighed just thinking about them.

Two sets of 12-foot-high, carved, wooden doors stand at the church entrance. The doors are extremely heavy and are held open by a chain that anchors them to the floor. The archdiocese didn't want a couple of hundred-pound doors closing on one of the grammar school children, so each day the parish priest releases the doors, locks them, and closes the church for the evening, just like he would do shortly. Churches used to be open 24/7, but for Saints Peter and Paul, the combination of homelessness and a series of church bombings in 2014 ended that particular tradition. Now Saints Peter and Paul, along with most other churches in the city, keep 'bankers' hours.

He waits patiently for one schoolgirl in particular. She IS different. She wears her hair in a pixie cut and swishes it around like she knows damn well the effect it has. Her look isn't innocent like most of the other girls. She seems older, somehow more experienced. After school, away from the nuns, she will roll her waistband, shortening her skirt. Then, from somewhere inside her white uniform blouse, she will pull out a cigarette and light up. The girl is always joined by two other girls, often offering them cigarettes. She is generous. He likes that.

He is getting aroused just thinking about her. And glad for his baggy white coveralls.

Only one problem - she hasn't shown up yet. Other contractors and workers are walking into and out of the church, and he frequently had to 'strike a pose,' looking like he is working, to not look suspicious. It is easy enough to look like he belonged there, with his coveralls, but still, he is getting nervous.

Glancing repeatedly at his watch, he decides to go back inside to paint the interior trim of the church baseboard, doorways, etc., the job for which he'd been hired. For ten days, it's been 'business as usual.' He can frequently leave the other contractors to do the bulk of the priming while he scouts.

There isn't much left to do. As the others finish, the final trim, his job, is all that remains. One of his vans, his capture van, is parked in back of the church; he needs the cover provided by a van. Tomorrow, the last official day of the job, he will bring the real van, the true company van. It looks exactly like the one he drives today, but had actual painting supplies in it.

He hasn't been able to do as much as he wanted — he is too excited. Because of that, he is going to need a little more time tomorrow to do the remaining touchup before he leaves the job for good. He doesn't like finishing mid-week, but it will be a full day, and then he'll be gone. He is going back inside basically to stall and to make an appearance. His brushes and rollers are all cleaned. All that is left on his 'to do' list is cleaning out a couple of almost empty five-gallon buckets.

Looking down at his watch again, he sees an hour has passed. "Shit!" he mutters, then looks around self-consciously. He doesn't know what the other contractors think about his swearing in a church, but fortunately they are in other parts of the building. Nobody is around.

He looks down toward the sidewalk and then up toward the school, his nerves on edge. If she doesn't show up today, it is all over. He has to bring the real van tomorrow, packed full of tools and painting supplies, which won't work for his purposes.

As his stomach began to churn in panic, a sense of relief suddenly comes over him. Her friends, he can see her two friends. He leans around the pillar, scanning the area, but she isn't there. His relief vanishes and he groans in anguish. He has so counted on her. He is tremendously disappointed, but he prides himself in his adaptability. One of her friends will have to do.

He is just about to turn back into the church when a car pulls up to the curb beside them. He watches as the girls lean over to speak to the driver, and feels a surge down below when their skirts ride up in the back. Yeah, one of them will do just fine.

His heart sinks when one of the girls reaches for the door handle, and they both slide into the car. As his face screws up in anger, he lets out a frustrated growl and kicks the pillar.

Muttering expletives under his breath, he turns and walks back inside. All the planning, the patiently waiting, the wonderful anticipation, is gone. Looking at the area behind the altar, he despondently inspects the work. He thinks about finishing up now, and not even bothering with coming back tomorrow. But he can't concentrate on it. He violently rubs both hands over his face, frustrated. He looks at his watch again and is surprised to see how much time had passed since he walked back into the church. It's after four o'clock; he's wasted almost an hour. He shakes his head. He is done for the day.

He bends over, picking up the five-gallon buckets. He sighs as he starts walking toward the side door where his van is parked, glancing toward the open front doors — he catches his breath. He can't believe his luck. One of the friends, the taller one, is sitting on the front steps of the church eating something. He stands quietly for a few moments, watching her. She isn't quite as mature looking as her friend, the one he wants. She is kind of skinny, a little gawky, but unquestionably pretty. And he has to admit that he feels the desired effect seeing her with her skirt gathered above her thighs.

She finishes whatever she is eating, and prepares to stand up. Now he looks around quickly, trying to decide what to do. Can he still complete his plan? He pivots on his heel, the nearly empty buckets in his hands swinging wildly, and heads back up the center aisle, turning toward the side exit door. Based watching over the last several days, he knows she will walk past right here. As she turns the corner, he lets his arms hang down to his sides, and feigns struggling out the door under the make-believe weight of the buckets.

"Hey!" he calls out tilting his head toward the van. "Can you do me a favor and pull that door open all the way? My hands are full."

She looks around, momentarily suspicious, or at least cautious. Smart girl. Then, he sees a look settle over her face, the look he had hoped for. He is coming out of the church. He's a painter working in the church: therefore, he must be all right.

"Sure," she says. She takes hold of the handle, pulling the door all the way open on its track.

"Thanks," he gasped believably, struggling to set the buckets down inside.

After a quick glance around, and seeing no one, he pulls a cloth out of his pocket, along with a little squeeze bottle. In one deft motion, he pops the top and squeezes, he then turns to the girl as if to say thank you and presses the now moistened cloth over her face. She grapples with him initially, but he grabs her by the back of the neck, keeping the cloth over her mouth and nose. She weakens quickly, and he eases her down into the back of his van. With one last look around, he slips in after her, pulling the door closed.

He yanks the lid off one of the buckets and pulls out a couple zip ties, binding her wrists and ankles. He feels his breath quicken as his hands grasp and position her legs. He pauses, his fingers caressing her smooth skin. He shakes his head. Not now. He has to wait.

Quickly, he reaches into the bucket again and grabs a couple rags. He crumbles one of them up and stuffs it into her mouth, securing it with another rag, tied around her head. She is still unconscious as he slips into the driver's seat, still not believing his good luck, and drives away.

She is terrified. Her wrists and ankles are sore where the zip ties dig into them. So is her body, from rocking around with the motion of the van. The gag in her mouth tastes like what she imagined paint would taste like, and the effect is only reinforced by the smell of the other rag tied around her head to hold it in, just below her nose.

There was something over her head, a hood of some kind, and it seems old and worn. She can see glimpses of light and shapes in a certain area if she turns her head exactly right. Lying on a drop cloth in the back of the van, her head was positioned behind the driver's seat. Though dark, she can occasionally see passing buildings or other structures through the passenger side window, but only if there are streetlights. With her knowledge of the city, even with her limited view of the passing structures, she guesses they are heading toward the Presidio.

Just before reaching the Golden Gate Bridge entry, the van turns off the main road and drives through the old Presidio Army base. She thinks she recognizes the Lucas Digital Arts buildings. Finally, they bounced into what seemed like a parking lot, maybe near one of the old gun emplacements. The van makes a few turns, apparently to maneuver into a particular location.

Then the engine shuts off and she hears the driver's door open and close.

Her heart is racing as the side door slides open. She knows the man is there in front of her, but she can't see him. "Come on," he says. "I'll get you out of there now."

She feels his hand wrap around her upper arm and pulls her toward the door. She doesn't know whether she should fight him or cooperate. She needs to be out of the van, but will fighting make any difference? Not being able to see will certainly hinder any escape attempt.

He helps her into a sitting position on the floor of the van, with her legs out the door, her feet on the ground.

"I'm going to take the ties off your ankles so you can walk," he says, but then his voice takes on a cold, warning tone. "But if you try to run, they go back on. Maybe worse. Got it?"

She shakes her head, yes, tears streaking down her face inside the hood.

"Good girl," he replies. He bends down, and she feels cold metal briefly touch her ankle. Then she feels the zip tie pop loose as the knife cut through the nylon tie, and her ankles are free.

It seems especially dark, so dark that the places worn thin on the hood don't do her any good. She hears the man stand back up and move something that sounds like a heavy plastic bag. She hears him pull out what may be another plastic bag — if that's what it is — from behind her, and then what sounds like fabric, perhaps a drop cloth.

"Come on," he says, his hand tightly grasping her upper arm. "Just cooperate and you can go home."

Her ankles are aching, but she stumbles along beside him. After a few steps, the sound changes, as if their footsteps are echoing inside a tunnel. The man stops and pulls the hood off her head. As she tries to adjust her eyes to the darkness of the passageway, he pushes her forward. They finally walk to where a dim light is mounted up high on a wall, then they stop.

He pulls her head in front of him. She looks, and through the distortion of her tears, she can see his eyes are hard and cold. "If I take the gag out," he says, "you can't yell or scream. If you do, I promise you'll be sorry."

She nods and he turned her around. Happy for any measure of relief, she feels the knot loosen, then come off. He pulls the crumbled up rag out of her mouth.

When she can finally speak, her words flood out in a torrent. "Why are you doing this?" she sobs. "I never hurt you. I don't even know you." Despite the sneer that forms on his face and the cold eyes, she continued imploring. "Please let me go home. I won't tell anyone about this. I promise!"

"You're just like all the rest of them," he says. "Going to your fancy school in your sexy little uniforms. You're just a bunch of teases, always thinking you're better than the rest of us, never giving us a second look."

"What?" she replied incredulously. "I'm not better than anyone, and my school isn't fancy. It's just the neighborhood Catholic school. Please just let me go!"

"No," he said, letting a slight smile playing about his lips. "I'm bringing you stuck-up little bitches to my turf. We'll see who comes out on top."

He tosses the drop cloth onto the ground and pushes her down on it. She looks up at him in terror as he pulls a knife out of his pocket and unfolds it. As the blade cuts through the fabric of her skirt, then her underwear, she clamps her eyes shut...

Finished, he stands and zips his pants up while looking down at his humiliated catch with satisfaction. She is curled up in a fetal position now, crying, trying to hide and cover herself. He smiles as he re-lives the feel of her body against his. As he pulls the long zipper to close his coveralls, she looks up at him. He can see something on her face, a sudden flash of anger overcoming the fear, recognition that since he'd already lied and done his damage, now any further compliance won't alter her chances of getting home.

"I understand now why you can never make it with girls," she seethed. She sat up, her lips curled in disgust. "We're out of your class! And I don't just mean us Catholic girls. Any girls are out of your reach. Without that knife, you wouldn't be able to get within a hundred feet of any of us. You're nothing but a pathetic fucking loser!"

His heart pounded against his chest, those old feelings coming up again, anger, rejection, and resentment. Along with quickened breathing, the uncontrollable impulse to lash out. He punches her in the face, and she falls over backwards. He kneels down, straddling her, and hits her again, then wrapping his hands around her throat, he squeezes. Though weakened and dazed by the blows, she struggles, trying to fight him off. He grabs her flailing arms and moves up a bit, pinning them down with his knees.

She takes a deep breath and starts to scream, but his hands tightened around her throat again, silencing her. He squeezes until she goes still, watching her bulging, accusing eyes.

As the adrenalin slowly dissipates, he gasps until his breathing returns to normal. He stands up and feeling as if he were coming out of a fog, he bends over and picks up the pieces of clothing he cut off her, and places them in the second of the large plastic bags. Next, he works the opening of the bag over the girl's body and rolls her into it.

The drop cloth goes into the first bag, along with the zip ties. He rolls it up and slips it under his arm, then grasping the other bag with both hands, he drags it toward the van. He struggles with the dead weight, and grins at the appropriateness of that phrase. Once at the van, he places both bags in the back and closes it up. He heaves a sigh of relief as he slips into the driver's seat and is now behind the wheel. He starts up the van and works his way back to the street.

Heading eastward on Clement Street, he eventually comes to Lincoln Park Golf Course. Knowing that nobody will be there at night, he drives in, making his way to the parking lot near the Legion of Honor Art Museum. The museum is closed, the parking lot empty. He has been to the museum before, on one of his scouting trips. The museum has cameras, but they all faced the museum and its entry points. The parking lot and its perimeter are unguarded.

After parking in one of the outer spaces near the golf course, he drags the girl's body out of his van and stashes it in some bushes surrounding one of the greens. Back at the van, he strips off his gloves and coveralls and stuffs them into the other bag.

He gets back in the van and drives out of the parking lot, preparing to turn back onto Clement Street. Then a sound, something rattling across the ridged floor of his van, thumping against the wall. He pulls over and slides the side door open. He feels around and finds it: a cell phone. He has never seen it before. It must be hers. He has seen enough cop shows to know that a cell phone can be traced to its present location. He needs to get rid of it. He bristles at the delay, but it has to be done. He is glad he found it.

He is headed down Columbus Avenue, driving toward the school and church where he had spent so much time over the last several days. Stopping at Washington Square Park, he takes an empty coffee cup from his cup holder, along with some wrappers from his lunch, and drops them, along with the phone, into a trash can. The phone will mark the girl's last known location. The police will assume she must have dropped it and someone threw it in the trash.

He looks around. Nobody is anywhere near, except a few homeless derelicts. He is home free.

CHAPTER 3

Liam is standing on his front porch with a travel mug in each hand when John pulls up. Liam steps down toward the curb and John reaches over and opens the passenger door.

Like John, Liam is also a 17-year veteran of the San Francisco police force and the product of the parochial school system, as are what seem like half of the police department.

Now 39, Liam is a divorced and fallen-away Catholic with no children and a string of failed and disastrous relationships behind him, with alimony looming in his future unless one of his exes decides to remarry. And that prospect doesn't look any too promising, as both are smart enough not to do anything foolish that will turn off the spigot. He lives by himself in a neat, old flat that has been renovated and brought up to current earthquake requirements, and then converted to a condo. He drives a three-year-old Porsche, the sole survivor of his latest divorce. Currently, he's been with Kathy, Inspector Sullivan, for almost two years.

"Good morning," Liam says as he pulls his door closed and fastens his seat belt. "I trust your drive in from suburbia was uneventful." John checks over his shoulder and pulls back into the street.

Like Liam, John is an Irish Catholic and a product of the city's parochial school system; he attends church semi-regularly. Inspector John O'Neill is a thirty-eight-year-old, a legacy SFPD officer, following his father and grandfather in the 'family business'. He has been on the job for fifteen years, the last five in homicide. John lives in Novato, in Marin County, north of San Francisco. He lives in a comfortable four-bedroom house with his wife of nearly 17 years and two children — a 15-year-old son and a 13-year-old daughter. John's wife Susan is a seventh-grade teacher in Novato.

It is a good marriage. They have remodeled their house over the years and now own an unbelievably valuable piece of real estate; however, thanks to the Bay Area's housing market and skyrocketing prices, they could not relocate anywhere else in the area. So, they are happy with what they have, even though the commute had become increasingly arduous.

One of the perks of working in Homicide is taking the company car home. Usually, the company car goes to the partner who drives the greater distance. Since John lives in Novato, about thirty miles north of the city, he has the car. The car is assigned to the team and the one with the greater distance to drive takes it home and then picks up his/her partner. The take home car is one of the perks to working homicide and being on-call 24/7, for each rotation. Since John lives in Novato, he picks up Liam on his way to the office.

Novato is basically considered a nice suburb of San Francisco, and home to about 600 San Francisco police officers and firefighters. The large population of civil servants resulted from an attempt made years ago to force the police and fire personnel to live in the city. The courts ruled that attempt illegal, but allowed the city to place mileage restrictions on police and fire personnel because of callback requirements. All parties in the lawsuit finally agreed on a 30-mile limitation. They put a compass in the center of the city and drew a circle, identifying the available areas for real estate purchases. Novato was in Marin County, had great weather and good schools, and sat right at the 30-mile limit. It fit the criteria perfectly, so a significant number of police officers and firefighters moved up north.

For the last three years, since John joined the Homicide Bureau, Inspector Liam Donnelly has been his partner.

Liam's question finally registers with John. "Sorry, just the usual number of idiots texting, putting on their makeup, and reading the paper. Oh, and my favorite, the assholes driving in the commute lane even though they're the only person in the car."

Liam smiled and nodded his head in agreement. "Why doesn't the CHP start citing those miscreants? I'm sure the fines will more than pay for the effort."

"I think it really comes down to the danger factor."

"Explain."

"Well, CHP traditionally uses the Motor Cops to work the commute lanes, and these poor bastards have to get through traffic to find the violator, then light them up and try to move them from the number one lane, across four or five lanes of traffic to the right shoulder," John says. "If they're successful and don't get killed in the process, they issue the citation and, in the time it takes them to accomplish this death-defying feat, ten more one-passenger cars go by." John is getting agitated just talking about it. "It's really risk versus reward, and I don't blame them for avoiding the risk."

"Yeah, I suppose that makes sense," Liam says, taking a sip of coffee. "So, how about this: Cal Trans places cameras on the overpasses above the commute lanes and snaps a picture of every car between 6:30 and 9:30 a.m. Then, one of their computer whiz kids puts a filter on the photos, culling out the one-person cars, and the violators are mailed a citation. You cite every violator, and the poor Motor Cops get to go back to whatever it is they do otherwise. At – what is it, $400 per cite? My little program would generate quite a windfall for the state."

"You know," John says, his eyebrows bunched together in thought, "as much as I hate to admit it, that actually makes a lot of sense. Catch the violator, free up the commute lanes, collect the fines, and hopefully keep a CHP officer from getting killed."

"That's high praise, coming from you," Liam replies. "I think I'll write my Assembly person."

"So, where is Inspector Sullivan this fine Tuesday morning?" John asked.

"She went back to her place. She has the company ride, and she has to pick up her partner on the way in this morning."

"You guys ever consider the crazy notion of living under one roof?"

Liam glances at him uncomfortably. "It's complicated. We both have our own places, so one of us would have to give up that failsafe, fallback location. What if things don't work out? One of us would be without a place to live."

John swallowed a gulp from his mug. "Good point. Good coffee, by the way. Since I didn't see Kathy's car, you must have been the one to push the 'brew' button on the Keurig."

"I am," Liam nodded proudly. "In fact, I even filled the reservoir with water and popped in the K-cup!"

"Amazing!"

CHAPTER 4

Sitting in his usual seat at the Homicide Bureau conference table in the San Francisco Hall of Justice, Liam half-listened to John's continued complaints about the hardened scofflaws in the commute lane. He glances across the table at Kathy. She is listening to something Reggie is telling her, but she catches Liam's glance.

The SFPD Homicide Bureau is located in Room 450 of the Hall of Justice, at 850 Bryant Street, in a building that opened in 1958. The entire police department used to be in the building, along with the Coroner, Courts, Jail, District Attorney's office, and Southern Station. The building was obsolete before the grand opening and ribbon cutting. More recently, the Administrative Offices and Southern Station were moved to a new location on Third Street, in Mission Bay, and a new jail was built. But the Investigations Bureaus and Traffic remained. Homicide sits exactly where it did when the Hall of Justice first opened. The building is old, gray, utilitarian, and pretty much without charm. The smart money said it won't survive even a medium-sized earthquake. It is too expensive to retrofit, and although new buildings are planned, they are well into the future... so it remains in place. The good news? When the other divisions left, the parking opened up!

Before any words can be exchanged, Lieutenant Daniel Lee enters the room and closes the door. Lieutenant Lee, known as Danny to his close associates and friends, is a 25 year SFPD veteran, the last seven as head of the Homicide Bureau. He is a second-generation Chinese American who has successfully worked several assignments in the department, finally earning his shot as head of Homicide. He grew up in Chinatown, and attended Galileo High School.

Galileo is the public high school for both North Beach and Chinatown, two neighborhoods separated by a single street — and about 1,000 years. At Galileo he was not only a top student, but also an All-City second baseman; the last such Galileo star was O.J. Simpson. Because of Danny's exceptional grades, coupled with his baseball prowess, he was awarded a full scholarship to the University of San Francisco (USF), San Francisco's Jesuit University. USF had been a football and basketball powerhouse in the '50's, and during that time, the Dons produced such football notables and NFL Hall of Famers as Ollie Matson, Gino Marchetti, Bob St. Clair, and Burl Toller, along with NBA Hall of Famers, Casey Jones, Fred Scolari, and Bill Russell. Scolari is probably the least known nationally, but since he is from

North Beach, and attended Galileo, he is the second most famous pro player from the neighborhood, the first being Joe DiMaggio.

Because USF is a feeder university for the Catholic high schools in the city, Danny made a number of friends from those schools, which served him well in the police department. He is either an honorary Italian or Irishman, depending on the holiday. He's known as a smart and seasoned investigator who treats the Inspectors like co-workers, not subordinates, and is never afraid to jump in and get his hands dirty. His office is at the end of the Homicide Bureau proper, past the interrogation rooms.

The voices quiet down as Lee stands at the head of the table to begin their weekly staff meeting. "Well, it's a new week," he starts, "and our fine citizens have only managed to kill off one of the population over the weekend. Harry, Chris, why don't you bring us up to speed on this latest?"

Inspectors Harry Johnston and Chris Dominguez have been assigned the case. "Just a simple case of marital discord," Harry says with a dismissive wave of his hand. "It started as a misunderstanding on the part of the wife concerning her husband's hobby. Apparently, he has a penchant for Russian hookers. It concludes with her deciding to deal with this 'offending serpent,' as she called him, by cutting off the heads of the snakes, both snakes, literally and figuratively. Hubby is now on tables three and four in the morgue."

"It's not going to be a very complex case," Chris adds. "She declined an attorney and insisted on telling us how she had tried to live with the situation, and his numerous promises to give up the hookers."

"His own version of *Eastern Promises*," Liam said. When a collective groan sounded around the room, he held up his hands in surrender, as if he didn't understand the reaction.

"As I was saying, Momma just couldn't live with the cheating any longer, so she waited until hubby was asleep and stabbed him right through the heart," Chris continued. "Then she removed the offending appendage."

"That must have been a mess," Reggie said.

"Messy, but not as bad as it could have been. Since she stabbed him first, his heart had quit pumping before she removed the rest. If that had been in reverse order— "

"—Okay, thanks for sharing," Lieutenant Lee interrupts with a roll of his eyes. "Maybe we can get back to pertinent information about our ongoing cases." He looks at Reggie and nods.

The detectives spend the next hour updating Danny and the others concerning open cases, both under investigation and in trial. After they were finished, they filed out of the conference room and went back to their respective desks, many of them to the never-ending drudgery of paperwork.

"Homicide? Isn't that jumping the gun?"

Lieutenant Lee had been relaxed until the phone call from the Chief's office. He leaned forward over his desk, the phone pressed to his ear, listening intently, his face lined with tension. "Well, I just mean that she's only been gone overnight. She's not even officially a missing person yet."

Liam hears the strain in Danny's voice through his open door. He's tuned into the conversation while keeping his eyes on the papers in front of him.

"The Archbishop? How is he involved?" A pause. "Saints Peter and Paul Church, yes, sir, I know it. Over by Washington Square, but —" Danny glances out through his door. "—No, I didn't know that is your parish. Well, I guess that explains the Archbishop . . . No, sir, I assure you I'm taking this very seriously. I'll get a team on it immediately . . . Yes, of course, I mean teams. Yes, sir. Good day, Chief."

Danny hangs up the receiver and sighs. Then, he stands and walks to the door. "John and Liam, Reggie and Kathy, my office. Now."

He paced back and forth, his head down in thought, as the four detectives filed into his office and stood expectantly in front of his desk. Danny looked up at them. "It seems we have a missing 14-year-old girl in North Beach, an eighth grader at Saints Peter and Paul Grammar School."

"Wouldn't that be—" John starts.

"And before you point out, correctly," Danny nods toward John, "that this is most assuredly a Missing Persons case, let me add the fact that Saints Peter and Paul Church is Chief Walker's parish, and the Archbishop is currently standing on the Chief's desk."

"Then it sure sounds like a Homicide case to me, boss," Liam said. "The story is that the girl called her mother yesterday afternoon after school, upset that she had received detention for what she perceived to be a minor infraction.

You'll have to talk to the good sisters to find out what nefarious activity this young woman is involved in. Evidently, Mom told her to calm down, that she could go to Victoria's for a pastry, and they could discuss the issue over dinner.

"Only she didn't come home. The Sector Car took the initial call and correctly pointed out that it wouldn't be a Missing Person, again, officially, for twenty-four hours. But Dad is a firefighter at Station 2 over on Powell, and they processed the case immediately. He was at the firehouse, but he's back home now."

The detectives glanced nervously at each other. Missing kids always made for delicate cases.

Danny pressed on. "Liam and John, I want you to go to the school and find out exactly what the hell happened to upset this young lady, then check Victoria's and see if she took Mom up on the pastry offer. Kathy and Reggie, go to the girl's house on Edith Street and interview the parents and any other kids. Let's get a picture of this young woman, see exactly who she is. And let's hope to hell she went to her girlfriend's house because she is in trouble at school."

The detectives nodded their understanding. "When you're done, let's plan to meet back here at 2:00. That will give me time to hear what you have to say and still have time to update the Chief," Danny added.

"Yes, sir," the detectives said in unison, as they filed out of the office.

They went to their desks to retrieve their jackets and keys. Reggie and Kathy headed off to the supply room for latex gloves, Tyvek suits, evidence bags, evidence tags, evidence flags, and anything else they might need, should this case go south. Liam and John are waiting at the elevator when Kathy and Reggie joined them.

"Wouldn't want to be in the Lieutenant's shoes on this one," Liam said. "Especially if it becomes a Homicide case."

"Don't even go there," John replied.

Kathy sighed in agreement. "Let's just plan on finding her at the girlfriend's house."

Kathy Sullivan is a 35-year-old veteran of twelve years with the SFPD. There is no denying she is an attractive woman who looks good without having to put a great deal of effort into her hair and make-up. She is tall with an athletic figure and strawberry blond hair that she ties back in a ponytail. Like John and Liam, she is also a product of the city's parochial school system. Judging by her last name, she may also be a member of the Irish Mafia at the SFPD. Kathy woke up in her house in the Sunset as she had gone home after work, rather than to Liam's condo. She would have much preferred she and Liam had a place together; but departmental rules preclude them being partners, and despite the relationship being common knowledge, cohabitating without the benefit of matrimony was still taboo in a number of circles at the PD. So, until Liam 'pops the question,' it is going to be musical beds.

Kathy is glad to have Reggie as her partner. Not only is he smart, but he also cuts an imposing figure as a former All-Pac 12 safety who once held pro football aspirations.

Strong as a bull and twice as fast, he is definitely someone to have on your side. While attending Lowell High School, the only San Francisco public school with an entrance exam, he earned a football scholarship to UCLA. A knee injury in the next to the last game of his senior year took him out long enough for the talent scouts to miss him. The injury healed, but he had to be satisfied with his degree in business.

Reggie's law enforcement career came about through the accidental death of a high school friend in a drive-by shooting. In his previous life, while in the corporate world, waiting for a conference call meeting, he listened as the others discussed the latest drive-by fatalities. They are concerned, they decry the violence, they shake their collective heads, and then go back to their P & L statements and what they cared most about, the bottom line. When he walked out of that meeting, he realized he did care, and he was determined to do something about it. He departs the business world and joins the Police Department. When he came to Homicide, he was assigned to be Kathy's partner.

Liam nods as the elevator doors slide open, but his lip is turned in a skeptical expression. He knows how often investigations go according to plan. He thought of the quotable Mike Tyson's famous words as a sports commentator told him of his next opponent's plan: "Everybody's got a plan — right up until I hit them in the face."

CHAPTER 5

Liam and John sit in hard chairs outside the principal's office at Saints Peter and Paul Grammar School. The grammar school is part of the parish, the church making up the balance of the property. The church is the center for San Francisco's North Beach Italian American community. Originally built in 1884, it was destroyed in 1906 by the Great San Francisco Earthquake, then rebuilt and re-opened in 1924. Administered by the Silesians of Don Bosco religious order, the church was originally known as 'la cattedrale italiana dell'Ovest,' or *the Italian Cathedral of the West*. Today, because of its proximity to Chinatown, it offers English, Italian, and Cantonese-language services. The grammar school, grades K-8, was established in 1925 and has served continuously since that date, the student body divided between children from both North Beach and Chinatown.

At the Principal's Office, John seems a little more relaxed than Liam. "What are you all hunched over for?" John asked.

Liam looked up at him with an inscrutable expression, "This just gives me the creeps."

John smiled, "Bad memories?"

"Oh yeah. Lots of 'em. I see a woman in black with a yardstick, and I still run."

A nun opened the door to the office. John could swear Liam jumped a little.

"Gentlemen, I'm Sister Mary Joseph. Please come in."

"Thank you for seeing us on such short notice," John says as they filed into the office after her.

"Of course, Lucia is one of our students and part of our family."

The detectives sit down in front of her desk, in chairs very similar to those they just vacated. "Sister, what kind of student is Lucia?" Liam asks.

"She's an above-average student. Not straight A's, but remarkably close."

"How about any issues involving discipline?" Liam continued. "We understand she received a detention recently."

"That's correct," Sister Mary Joseph replied. "She and two other girls were seen by one of our parents walking near Washington Square with their skirts rolled."

"I'm sorry," John leaned forward a little. "Their skirts rolled?"

"Yes. The uniform skirt is worn so that the hem is located just below the knee. A modest length. Some of the girls prefer a trendy look and want the hemline somewhere between the knee and the thigh. Completely wrong and just not allowed. So, they take the waistline and roll it up, thereby shortening the length of the skirt."

"Based on grades, it sounds like they were paying attention in math and English class," Liam says, apparently overcoming his childhood anxiety.

The principal's eyebrows raise in a scolding expression. "We take a very dim view of these shortened skirts, as do most of our parents."

"So, what happened to cause the detention?" John asked.

"I received a call from one of our parents who was coming from church, a ladies auxiliary meeting in the afternoon. She saw three of our girls standing on the corner, out of sight of the school, rolling their skirts; this despite our warnings to the contrary."

"Did this mother recognize all the girls involved?"

"No, she only recognized Lucia Rosini and Ann Perotti, both eighth graders here. She didn't recognize the third girl."

"What happened after this information reached your office, sister?" Liam asked.

"Lucia and Ann were called to my office and I confronted them with the information provided by our concerned parent. The girls admitted to rolling their skirts and said they did it to be more comfortable on their walk home."

"What about the third girl, the one your confidential informant couldn't ID?"

"I'm sorry, confidential informant?"

"Sorry, sister," Liam snickered. "Police term for a snitch."

"Sister," John quickly jumped in, "we just need to know the name of the third girl and where we might be able to find her."

"Well, neither Lucia nor Ann could recall who they were with that day," Sister Mary Joseph replied. "They say they frequently walk home with different girls, depending on everyone's schedule."

"I like these girls already," Liam said. "Sister, were either Ann or Lucia in trouble previously? Were they discipline problems?"

"I'm not sure where you're going with this," she replied a little suspiciously, "but neither girl has been in trouble before. They're both excellent students."

John cast a reproving look at Liam. "Sister, my partner is just trying to determine the identity of the third girl by association, if either Ann or Lucia has been in trouble before."

"Oh, I see."

"Is detention considered a serious discipline?" John asked.

"Yes, it is. It won't become a permanent mark on their record, providing they do not have any further negative contacts for the rest of the year."

"So, you take two young girls," Liam pondered, "both, I assume, products of the whole Saints Peter and Paul Grammar School experience, now in the eighth grade, preparing for high school next year..." He looked pointedly at the principal. "A competitive process, I believe?"

"Yes."

John began to fidget in his chair.

"And, just for the record, you take these girls, who have no history of discipline and who are in your words, 'excellent students,' and on the word of a nosy parent coupled with the girls' honest response to your questions, you punish them with discipline that would make them two strikers in our system." Liam paused to let it sink in. "Doesn't that seem a bit excessive to you?"

"Oh boy," John groaned.

"I really don't see how your questioning our long-established procedures will bring you any closer to locating Lucia," Sister Mary Joseph retorted.

"It may not, but it may explain her reasons for running in the first place." Liam shot a smartass smile at her. "Congratulations."

"Uh, sister, is Ann in class right now?" John asked.

"Yes, of course."

"What's your procedure for letting us talk to her?"

"I notify her teacher and bring her to my office. You may use the conference room if you like. Should I be present?"

"No, sister," Liam replied, "we'd prefer a candid and spontaneous conversation. Your presence will just intimidate the young lady."

John smiled awkwardly, adding, "But thank you for offering!"

Kathy and Reggie arrive at the Rosini home, where Mr. Rosini answers the door and invites them in. The house is a two-story, well cared-for, older San Francisco home. On the first floor are the living room (no one had a family room when the house was built), kitchen, dining room, and a renovated master bedroom, with the remaining bedrooms upstairs. The home is immaculate, with the requisite Crucifix on the living room wall, and generations of family photos on the mantle. The living room has a sofa, coffee table, and a couple chairs. There is a TV on a stand near the window. Kathy and Reggie are shown to the sofa and invited to sit; Mrs. Rosini offers coffee and biscotti. They decline the offer, saying they didn't want to waste any time. The Rosinis sit in the two occasional chairs.

"Mr. and Mrs. Rosini," Kathy begins, "has Lucia ever stayed out all night before?"

Mr. Rosini interjects, "please, it's Tony and Anna."

Kathy agrees, and they moved forward.

As they answer, Reggie covertly glances around the Rosini's living room, looking for clues in family photos. Sometimes old photos tell a different story, he thought… but not today. What he sees is a series of previous happy memories.

"No," Mrs. Rosini replies, worry etched across her face. "She's a good girl. She's never been in any trouble, always gets good grades, and helps out around the house. She wants to go to Saint Ignatius, to be the first girl in the family to attend SI."

"Lucia called you after school, isn't that correct?" Reggie asked.

"Yes, that's right."

"What exactly did she say?"

"She was crying. She received an hour's detention punishment because somebody saw her and two other girls rolling their skirts to shorten them. It's not allowed, but the girls do it to look a bit more stylish."

"Although I don't think anyone's going to be a fashion icon in a Catholic school girl's uniform," Mr. Rosini adds, "The girls don't mean anything by it. They're just rebelling. I did far worse when I was 14."

"Lucia was worried this detention would reflect badly on her and hurt her chances of getting into SI," Mrs. Rosini said. "She's worked so hard on her grades, and she should get in without any trouble."

Kathy smiled warmly, "I'm sure she will."

"I told her to stop crying and go to the little tin box in the kitchen drawer, take out some money for a nice pastry at Victoria's, and to walk over and get it. That would make her feel better until I could get home."

"What happened then?"

"I figured she'd be fine, so I went back to work. I'm the office manager at Scoma's on the Wharf. I get off at 5:30, I come home, and Lucia isn't here. I think she must have run into a friend on the way home and she will be back any minute, but she didn't show up, so I called my husband."

Mr. Rosini stood up and moved to the window. Then he adds, "I told her to check with some of her girlfriends to see if she went to one of their houses. It wouldn't be like her not to tell us, but kids can screw up. When we still hadn't heard anything by 8:00 p.m., we called you guys."

"Mrs. Rosini," Reggie said, "I assume you didn't get any useful information from the friends you called?"

"No, no one had seen Lucia since school."

"Can I get a list of the people you called, so we won't end up duplicating our efforts and wasting time?"

Mrs. Rosini nodded, "Of course."

"I was at the firehouse when the police arrived here," Mr. Rosini said. "2 Truck on Powell. My Captain called a replacement in early, and I got home just after the police arrived."

"The officers were very nice," Mrs. Rosini interjected, "and they explained about the 24 hour waiting period on missing persons."

"Then I got home, in uniform, and they bent all the rules. They took the report, they talked to the neighbors, they brought in extra cars," Mr. Rosini continued. "They were great, but no Lucia."

"Mrs. Rosini, may we look at Lucia's room?" Kathy asked.

"Of course," the worried mother replied.

"Absolutely." Mr. Rosini stood up and led them upstairs to the bedroom.

The detectives slowly walked around the room, looking at everything, while the parents stood in the doorway. Reggie notices posters of current teen heartthrobs (did they still call them that?) and stuffed animals. Kathy looks at the clothing, the tennis shoes and one-inch heels, the ankle socks, and nylons.

"Looks like a typical 14-year-old's room," Reggie said as they stand in front of a small desk in front of the window.

"I know," Kathy agrees. "All the trappings of someone on the cusp between childhood and womanhood." She notices all the items on the desk. "Reggie, I don't like this. Her laptop is here, her purse is here," she said quietly. She glanced at a pair of jeans draped over the back of the chair. "I don't think she even changed clothes."

"Hmm," Reggie grunted. "Look, here's a diary. I didn't know girls even kept diaries anymore. I thought they revealed everything on Facebook, Instagram, and Tik Tok."

"I think Lucia may be a bit of a throwback to a much better time," Kathy replied. She turned around to face the parents, still standing at the door. "Mrs. Rosini, can you confirm that Lucia didn't change clothes. Is she still wearing her uniform?"

"Yes, that's right. She usually changes into jeans and a T-shirt, but they're all still here."

"Can you tell me if anything is missing from her room? Anything at all?"

"No, I think everything is here, except her phone."

"I think the phone is permanently attached," Mr. Rosini joked, trying to hide his nervousness.

Reggie brightened up a bit. "Does the phone have a GPS locator on it?" he asked.

"I believe it does," Mr. Rosini replied. "Why didn't I think of that?"

"It's alright. You have a lot on your plate. That's why we're here. Who's the carrier?"

"AT&T."

Kathy nods. "Okay. Reggie and I are going to get in touch with the AT&T office to see if we can get the GPS activated. We'll call you as soon as we know anything." She looked into the worry on their faces. "In the meantime, I'm going to call the Police Chaplain's Office and have a volunteer priest assigned to your family. He can provide some support and encouragement while the search is going on."

"Thank you," Mrs. Rosini smiled weakly.

CHAPTER 6

Kathy is already working on getting through to the IT officer, so Reggie slid the driver's seat back so he could fit his legs under the steering wheel and drive. It is silent for a while as Kathy waits on hold for the IT person to pick up.

While heading south on Hyde Street, past the iconic houses, corner cafes and coffee shops, Reggie follows the cable car tracks embedded in the asphalt. He remembers the old Rice-A-Roni commercials, and how every one of them ended with a shot of a cable car traveling on Hyde Street.

"Hello," Kathy says, perking up, "this is Inspector Kathy Sullivan. I need to have a GPS tracker activated. The carrier is AT&T, the number is 415-600-0789." She pauses to listen to the number being read back to her. "Yes. We need to know where it is right now. Call me back on this number, okay? Thank you."

She disconnects and sits back with a sigh.

"So," Reggie said, "to the Lieutenant's office, right?"

"Yes, we need to bring him up to speed on this."

The conference room at Saints Peter and Paul Grammar School is dim, the table dark and old, but without a single mark or gouge on the top. Liam drums his fingers on it while he and John wait.

After Sister Mary Joseph opens the door, a girl walks in. She looks at both men, an expression just this side of fear on her face. John stands up and motions to a chair as the door closes.

"Ann Perotti?" he asks. She nodded as she sits down. "Hi, Ann." He sits back down and scoots his chair forward. "My name is John. This is my partner Liam. We're San Francisco Police officers. We're trying to find your friend, Lucia. She didn't come home last night, and we were hoping you might have some idea where she might be."

"I don't know," she says, her lip quivering as tears accumulated in her eyes.

"It's okay, Ann," John said. "You don't need to be afraid. Just tell us what you know."

She takes a deep breath and wipes her eyes. She looks at John and Liam, visibly upset.

"We both got in trouble yesterday," she started, her voice trembling. "We told the truth, but it didn't matter. Sister just gave us detention anyway. Neither of us has been in trouble before, and we both get good grades. Lucia and I have applied to Saint Ignatius, and now we have detentions on our records."

"I know," Liam agrees. "The whole detention thing seems a bit over the top to me. But can you tell us where you and Lucia went after school yesterday? And we'll need the name of the third girl who was with you on your infamous skirt rolling caper."

"Lucia and I left school together." Ann sits back in her chair, Liam's comment seeming to take the edge off. She breathed deeply and steadied her voice. "But since it was a little later than usual because of the detention, I called my Mom and she picked us up. We dropped Lucia off, then my mom and I just went home. Lucia wanted to get home because she needed to talk to her Mom about the detention." She looked imploringly at both detectives. "If I give you the name of the third girl, will you tell Sister?"

"Not a chance," Liam insists. "We'll even contact her after school hours, so Sister won't know."

Ann nods, relieved. "Her name is Claire, Claire Johnson. She had been given a detention earlier for rolling her skirt, and we knew she would be in big trouble." She glanced toward the door. "So, we couldn't remember the name."

"So, you guys are good friends. Can you give us her number and address so we can talk to her?"

"Sure."

"Ann, can you think of any reason why Lucia would run away?" John asked. "Did she get along with her parents, her brother and sister? Did she have a boyfriend?"

"Lucia would never run away. Her Mom and Dad are cool. You can talk to them. Lucia is the big sister; she loves her brother and sister. I know this may sound strange, but Lucia is happy, and this detention really upset her. It upset me too, but Lucia wanted to be the first girl in her family to go to SI. Lots of boys went there, but she is going to be the first girl. Not so much pressure on me, since my older sister is at SI now."

John smiled as he stood up. "Thanks, Ann. You've been a big help."

"I hope you can find her," Ann said as she walked toward the door. "I'm worried about her."

John gave her his most reassuring look. "I know. We'll find her."

As they opened the door, Ann walked past Sister Mary Joseph, her head slightly downcast.

"Sister," John said, "thanks for your help, and for the use of the room. Before we go, do you have a school picture of Lucia that's current?"

"I thought you might want one." She immediately hands over a photo. "This was taken only last month."

"And do you have the name of that concerned parent from the other day?" Liam asked.

"Yes. It's clipped to the photo."

"Thank you," John said. "We'll be in touch."

The Victoria Pastry Company was founded in 1914, as their black-and-white striped awning out front proudly declared. Standing less than a block away from Saints Peter and Paul Catholic Church and school, the San Francisco Italian Athletic Club, and Chinatown; a large percentage of their clientele is Italian, Catholic, and Chinese. The rest are from all over the city, and they just loved the famous pastries. As they entered the building, John and Liam are pleasantly assaulted by the sweet aromas. They stop in front of a huge display case offering only the Torts. There are similar display cases for cookies, cakes, and other delicacies. Liam, his mouth watering, is reading the list of Torts out loud: "Javier Tart Almond coffee cake in a tart shell with assorted jams and streusel crumbles... Cannoli, Sicilian pastries filled with sweetened ricotta cheese inside a crunchy shell... Napoleon Layers of puff pastry and vanilla custard... Torta de Nonna delicate pastry crust combined with cream, and flavored with lemon zest... Open Crostata, open-faced pie-like almond tart, with jam filling... Closed Crostata partially covered, pie-like tart, with jam topping..."

John grabs Liam's shoulder. "Before you drool on the counter, let's talk to someone about Lucia."

"Right, but do you see these things?"

"Behave and maybe I'll buy you one later."

"Thanks, Dad."

A young man looks at them expectantly from behind the counter. John makes a beeline for him. "Hello, I'm Inspector John O'Neill, and this is Inspector Liam Donnelly. We're with the San Francisco Police Department. Were you working yesterday afternoon?"

"Yes, I was. I worked from 9:00 a.m. to 5:00 p.m. yesterday."

John pulls the photo of Lucia from his jacket pocket. "Do you recognize this young woman?"

"Oh, yes, that's Lucia Rosini. She was in for a sweet yesterday at about 4:00. Nice girl, nice family."

"Are you sure about the time?" Liam asks.

"I'm not positive, but it was about 4:00, give or take a few minutes. I get off at five, and my feet were telling me it was quitting time."

"Do you remember what she ordered?"

"Of course, a Cannoli. That's her favorite."

Liam interjected. "Did she eat it here or take it to go?"

"She took it with her."

"Thank you. You've been a big help."

As the detectives turn to leave, the young man stops them. "Why are you asking about Lucia? Is she alright?"

"She didn't come home last night, and we're trying to find her." Liam waves his hand as if it were nothing to worry about. "She's probably at a girlfriend's house."

"I hope so, she's a good girl."

The detectives nod in agreement and take their leave. "I can't believe we just walked out of there without getting something," Liam says as they get in the car.

"Nobody's stopping you," John replied.

Liam looks back, then shakes his head and pulls his door closed. "Better not. I need to watch my figure."

John pauses before starting the car. He looks at Liam. "All joking aside, I don't like the way this one is shaping up."

"I know. I've got a really bad feeling about this whole thing."

"Why don't we go back and fill in the Lieutenant."

"Good idea. After that, school will be letting out. We can get in touch with Claire Johnson."

Kathy and Reggie are already in Lieutenant Lee's office when Liam and John arrive, their faces taut. Danny comes in right behind them.

"Sorry for the delay," he says as he walks around his light gray, utilitarian, government issued, hopelessly cluttered desk. "The Chief was hounding me for an update before I even had any information." He looked expectantly at them, "So, where are we?"

"This is looking more and more like an abduction," Kathy started. "Lucia left everything behind but her phone. I have our IT people working with AT&T to activate the GPS so we can locate it."

Danny shakes his head as John takes up the narrative. "The school came down pretty hard on two of the three girls involved in the capital offense of rolling up their uniform skirt above the knee after school. Thereby adding credence to the adage, 'there's no greater wrath than that of a petty bureaucrat discovering the mistake of another.' The second girl, Ann Perotti, is a good kid, too. She verified everything we know so far. Ann said that the Rosinis are great parents and that there's no disconnect between Lucia and her parents, or her brother and sister.

"The third girl is unknown to the school, but we have her information, and we'll talk to her later today, after school. We don't want to go to the school and shine a spotlight on her, and give the good sisters the girl's identity. Lucia went

45

to Victoria's around 4:00, just as her Mom told her, and the young guy behind the counter knew her and remembered seeing her."

Reggie jumped in. "The Dad is an SFFD firefighter assigned over at 2 Truck. The Sector car did all the right things and pulled out all the stops as soon as they knew the girl is a firefighter's daughter. A lot of what would have been our initial legwork was already done by patrol. Those two blue suits should get a nice letter when this is over."

"Good work," Danny says. "So, the last confirmed sighting we have on our girl is about 4:00 p.m. yesterday, as she leaves the bakery. After that it's a mystery. I think we should grab as many of our people as we can and get to Washington Square at 4:00 today and start talking to everyone who may have been in the area yesterday."

"That is going to draw a lot of attention," Liam pointed out. "I mean, it's absolutely the right thing to do, but I'd like to avoid the Mobile Command Post or a huge number of black and whites." It's like churning the water for the press.

"I know, and I agree. But I'm afraid we don't have the manpower here in Homicide to be discreet."

Liam's forehead is furrowed, lost in thought. Then the lightbulb lights, "What if you let the Chief know that this canvas will be instrumental in redirecting the Archbishop's desktop oratory back to the cathedral? Do you think he might be able to order up some additional bodies from Missing Persons, General Works, and Narcotics?"

"Narcotics?" Danny said, his eyes narrowed.

"Have you seen the clientele that hangs out in Washington Square Park? I think Narcotics is the only unit who can work that park without drawing a crowd."

"Good point." Danny thinks for a second. "Okay. I'll have someone coordinate the responding units until I get there. I'll brief the Chief, and I'll bring the roster of people he frees up. I'll bring one clerical person with me, and I'll set up shop in the Italian Athletic Club. They have rooms, and I know they'll let us use one. I'll make that our command post so we're off the street." He looked at John and Liam. "I know you have an interview set up now, so meet us there as soon as you're done."

"Got it," John says. "I think we should dump our cars at Firehouse 28 on Stockton, and then walk down to the search area. Everyone will be in plain clothes, except Narcotics. God only knows what they'll be wearing. I'll call 28 and set it up."

"This is going to generate a lot of paperwork, Lieutenant," Liam observed. "Can we take over the conference room for the night and tomorrow morning, so we have room to make sense of it all?"

"Absolutely. So, let's get going. We only have a few hours."

"I'll go to IT to check on the phone," Kathy said.

"Good. Keep me informed."

CHAPTER 7

"Any luck?" Kathy asks as soon as she enters the IT department.

The man at the counter reaches up and touches the Bluetooth earbud phone in his ear. "I was just going to call you. "We have AT&T on the phone, and they say the phone is stationary now, on Mission at 8th."

"Can you keep AT&T on the line?" Reggie asked urgently. "And have them stay on top of the phone?"

"Sure thing."

"Can they tell us where the phone has been?" Kathy asks.

"Yeah, if they have the phone and the SIM card."

Reggie touched Kathy on the shoulder. "You go tell the Lieutenant. I'll bring the car around front."

"Thank you!" Kathy said to the IT tech as they rushed out.

Lieutenant Lee is sitting behind his desk tilting his head, trying to stretch and relax the muscles in his neck. From the look on his face when Kathy rushes into his office, the stretching isn't successful.

"Lieutenant," she said breathlessly, "we have the phone at 8th and Mission. Reggie and I are on the way, so we may miss the festivities at Washington Square."

"Finally, some good news," he said. "Go find the phone and whoever has it. I'll let patrol know and have some black and whites respond. We can't let this guy get away." He reaches for his phone, then stops. "What does the phone look like? And what's the number?"

"Shit!" Kathy replied. "I have the number, but I didn't get a description of the phone."

"That's okay. Call her Mom and get the description. Call me when you get it, and I'll get it to the responding units."

"Thanks, Lieutenant. On my way."

As soon as her door is closed and Reggie takes off, Kathy is on her phone. "Mrs. Rosini, it's Inspector Kathy Sullivan. I hate to bother you but -"

"Have you found her?" Mrs. Rosini's voice is a quivering mix of worry and hope.

"No, I'm sorry, I don't have any new information, yet. But I was wondering if you could describe Lucia's phone to me."

"It's an iPhone, an iPhone 11 I think, and it has a pink Hello Kitty carrying case."

"Perfect. Oh, one more thing. if we do find the phone, does it have a password?"

"Yes," Mrs. Rosini replied, her voice cracking with emotion. "Catmandu. It's spelled with a C and not a K. That was Lucia's cat. She died last year."

"I'm sorry, but thank you. I'll call as soon as I have any news."

Kathy quickly calls Lieutenant Lee and gives him the description of Lucia's phone as Reggie pulls over near one of the four SFPD black and whites parked on Mission. Several uniformed officers stood on the sidewalk in a sea of people.

"Oh my god," Kathy whispered.

The sidewalk along the massive gray bulk of the Pacific Gas and Electric Company is nearly covered with sleeping bags and blankets, and even a few tents. The homeless encampment stretches for nearly two full blocks. They get out of the car and approach, their eyes scanning the crowd. The smell is pretty much what Kathy expected from a sidewalk covered with homeless people, some with dogs, littered with garbage, rotting food, cigarette butts, needles, and occasional deposits of dog shit. At least she hoped it was dog shit.

With her phone pressed against her ear, she listened for a moment to the IT tech, and then spoke up to the officers. "AT&T says the phone is on the north side of Mission, between 8th and 9th."

One of the officers spread his arms, motioning toward the block-long area they were already searching. "Well, that really narrows it down," he said. Kathy looked at his nametag. 'Cookson,' it read.

"Sorry. They can only zero in on an approximate area."
She listened again. "Okay, closer to 8th, probably within a
hundred feet."

Reggie, Kathy, Cookson, and the other uniformed officers
scanned faces and body language, looking for anything suspicious. They noticed a man cramming things into his sleeping bag. His face an expression of exaggerated nonchalance,
while his body moved frantically.

"Hey, partner," Cookson said, approaching the man,
"Whatcha doin'?"

"Nothing, just moving my stuff out of the way." The "s"
sounds whistled between his missing teeth.

"You wouldn't happen to have a phone in there, would
you?"

"Do I look like I can afford a phone?"

"That's not what I asked," Cookson said, glancing over at
Reggie and Kathy. "I asked if you have a phone."

"Yeah, I got a phone," he replied with a tone of resignation.

He reached into a pocket and pulled out a 20-year-old
flip phone. The upper portion, the part with the screen, is
cracked, and one side of the hinge is broken. It's likely years
since it has been powered up.

"Any other phones?"

"No." The man held his head up defiantly, pushing strings
of greasy hair away from his face. His defiance faltered
quickly as he looked up at Officer Cookson. "You're not going search me, are you?"

"Well, I don't have probable cause." He looked toward Reggie, his face displaying a subtle grin, "Yet."

Reggie nodded as he pulled out his phone. He had already entered Lucia's number, just after they had gotten it from her mother, and he pressed the contact.

"I hope you're ready to run if it rings," Reggie said to Cookson.

As the call went through, they heard a muffled ringtone. Reggie turned his head a little, to try to pinpoint the sound. When he looked down toward the foot of the sleeping bag, the man reached for it, trying to quickly gather up his things, but Officer Cookson grabbed his arm, restraining him.

Reggie picks up the end of the sleeping bag, holding it up on a bit of a slant. A pink iPhone slides out onto the sidewalk. "Hello, Kitty!"

Reggie smiles as he snapped his gloves on. He picks up the phone and slips it into an evidence bag just as Officer Cookson fastened handcuffs around the homeless man's wrists. The other uniformed officers witnessed the questioning and the subsequent arrest and gathered around to help secure the area.

Kathy dialed into the office. "Lieutenant," she said as soon as Danny picked up, "we have Lucia's phone. Some homeless guy had it in his sleeping bag. Don't know how he got it, or how he fits into the whole scheme of things, but he's in custody on his way to the Hall."

"Good work!"

"It was the patrol officers. I don't know how they deal with this sort of thing every day."

"They'll get commendations," Danny says, "as soon as I get time."

"I have a feeling this guy isn't going to be the person we're looking for," Kathy continues, "so I think the stop-and-talk at the Square is still our best chance. We'll get this phone to the IT people and see if we can track Lucia's movements up until she lost it. We're just lucky this idiot didn't turn it off or remove the battery."

"He is probably just thrilled it worked," Danny said. "He wouldn't want to risk turning it off. It'll be interesting to see who he's called while he had it."

Kathy sighed. "We're on it. We're also in the process of collecting all our suspect's worldly possessions to see if there might be any clues in this portable landfill."

"Okay. I'm off to see the Chief and then to the Square." Kathy heard strain in Danny's voice and a rub of fabric. She imagined him holding the phone against his shoulder as he pulled his jacket on. "Keep me in the loop if this guy offers anything tangible."

"Will do, sir."

CHAPTER 8

Chief Michael Walker is a 32-year veteran of the department and has worked every detail on his way up the career ladder. Now at 55, he has served six years as the Police Chief, quite an accomplishment in as politically diverse a city like San Francisco. He is on his second mayor, still viewed by City Hall as an effective leader, and approaching a well-deserved retirement date.

He still hasn't decided on the exact date, so he isn't yet a member of the KMA (Kiss My Ass) Club. That exclusive enclave belonged to those with the requisite number of years for their pension, coupled with sufficient years to vest that pension, making it yours, no matter what. Once there, with this newly acquired 'bullet proof' status, he would be presented the opportunity for 'very frank' discussions with the city politicos. He is currently popular among the members of the department, but that popularity would rise and fall with any discipline he might be forced to mete out. Popularity is fleeting.

"And this homeless guy?" Chief Walker asked after Lieutenant Lee finished relating the day's developments on the case.

"Probably sitting in an interrogation room by now, waiting to be interviewed."

"Good…"

He is about to say more, but his phone rings. He holds up his index finger, the understood gesture to wait, and picks up the receiver. "Chief Walker." He listens for a moment. "Hold on, Lieutenant Lee is in here with me. I'm going to put you on speaker." He presses a button and hangs up the receiver. "Go ahead."

"Okay, this is Melissa Rossi, one of the departmental Press Information Officers." The PIO's voice sounded a little tinny over the phone's little speaker. "We're starting to get some questions from the more seasoned members of the press wanting to know about a roust of a large homeless camp on Mission at 8th. Also, a couple of the brighter ones noticed that Homicide is on Mission as well, and one evidently has a source in the Fire Department, and she's asking about a possible missing person."

"Shit." The Chief kneads his tired eyes. "Can you buy us a little more time, Rossi? Maybe you can give them a story about an investigation into an out-of-the-area homicide. Tell them we were following a lead, looking for a possible witness. That could help explain Homicide being on Mission. Also, tell them you'll check on the missing person angle. But it will probably be tomorrow at the earliest before we have any answers. We're going to be in the Washington Square area in just a few minutes interviewing a lot of people and we don't need the press looking over our shoulders and conducting their own interviews."

"Okay, Chief, I understand. I'll throw down some sand and start dancing."

"Thanks." He presses the button, disconnecting the call. He sits back in his chair.

"Sounds like our window of opportunity is about to slam shut," Danny said ominously.

The Chief rubs his face and sighs. "Do what you can tonight," he says. "Conduct your interviews, shake up this homeless guy, trace the phone, and do whatever else you can squeeze in, because I think tomorrow, all hell's going to break loose."

"Well, at least you bought us 24 hours. Thanks, boss."

He just folded the last of the drop cloths after getting a later start than he had hoped. However, his ability to focus on the job is sharper than it had been yesterday. He got all the touchups done and, by 3:30, began loading up his van. The real van.

It is parked at the rear of Saints Peter and Paul Church. The logo and contact information painted on the outside of the van looks exactly the same as the van he'd driven the girl in, but inside this van, unlike the other, is packed to the roof with painting supplies and tools. He tosses the drop cloth into the back of the van, on top of the others, and closes the door. He takes a moment to pull a handkerchief out of his pocket and wipe the sweat from his face while reflecting on the past few days.

It had been a good job. He is happy with his work, and hoped the church would be, too. He is a professional. Yesterday's distraction notwithstanding, he took pride in his work.

All that is left now is to stop at the rectory and get his pay. He has requested payment in cash, and the Monsignor has been more than happy with the cash payment since it went with a reduced cost. With that agreement already in place, there will be no complications.

He walks to the rectory and rings the bell. He doesn't know anything about the Catholic Church, but in his short time working in one, he's figured out the priests live in the rectory. He made his deal with the older priest, who seemed to be in charge. He based this assumption on the man's age and his own time in the military. This older priest has purple trim on his black outfit, like a sergeant's stripes. He doesn't know for certain what his next move will be, but it will likely involve relocating. He has a feeling that things were about to get exciting. Maybe a little too exciting.

An older woman answers the door. He explains that he is the painter and he's there to pick up his pay. She invites him into an office just to the left of the front door and asks him to wait. About five minutes later, the older priest with the purple trim on his outfit enters the office. The priest hands him an envelope with the agreed-upon cash payment and thanks him for his excellent work. They shake hands and he walks out the front door and into his van. Once in the van, he drives back to Illinois Street.

Lieutenant Lee and a couple of SFPD staff begin setting up their command post in one of the small rooms at the Italian Athletic Club, across Stockton Street from Washington Square. Founded in 1917, the San Francisco Italian Athletic Club (SFIAC) is the heartbeat of the Italian community in San Francisco. Danny thinks he can detect the lingering aroma of Italian food, but he isn't positive. Nobody complained though; for many, it is just like home.

The building houses offices, a large auditorium, a bar, and meeting rooms on the first floor. The upstairs has banquet halls, another bar, meeting rooms, a gym, and storage. The smaller meeting rooms are usually reserved for committee meetings or luncheons. The SFIAC is just down the block from Saints Peter and Paul Church, and across the street, or a stone's throw from some of San Francisco's finest Italian restaurants.

You can take a five-minute walk from the SFIAC and pass Original Joe's in the remodeled former Fiore De Italia, continue on to The North Beach restaurant, San Francisco's oldest Italian restaurant, and then turn the corner onto Green Street and walk past Café Sport, where the Sicilian meals didn't cheat you on garlic, and the wait staff insult you if you linger too long. Danny, having grown up on the other side of Columbus Ave., in Chinatown, still loved the North Beach cuisine.

Columbus Avenue is the dividing street between Chinatown and North Beach. If you walked east on Columbus Ave, it also affords a glimpse into a part of San Francisco's storied past. Columbus Avenue and Broadway Streets were the epicenter of the topless dancing movement in the 60's, and the location of some of the most famous nightclubs of that era. The Roaring 20's, Big Al's, and the Condor were the most notable, with the Condor and Carol Doda as the front-runner. Doda was arrested in 1965 for dancing topless; however, the judge issued a directed "Not Guilty" verdict, stating, "Whether acts ... are lewd and dissolute depends not on any individual's interpretation or personal opinion, but on the consensus of the entire community..." The community said it was OK. The clubs later surrendered the turf to cheap strip clubs and sleazy bars. The consensus of the entire community had shifted... a far cry from the 60's.

CHAPTER 9

At the SFIAC, a man poked his head in the door. "How's it going?" he asks Danny. "Will this suit your needs?"

"Yes, it will work just fine," Danny replies. "Thank you, Lorenzo."

Lorenzo, the club president for the past five years, and a fixture for more than 40, is a composite of Pavarotti and Santa Claus.

"I really appreciate you letting us use your place. We couldn't have run this operation out on the street without drawing way too much attention from the press," Danny said.

Lorenzo shook his head. "Happy to help. That little girl is from the neighborhood. Anything we can do to help, just say the word."

"There is one thing. Is there a back or side door we can use so we're not going through the front of your place all evening?"

"Yes, there's a door in the rear that leads directly into this room."

"Perfect. Thanks again, Lorenzo."

"We have a membership meeting in the main hall, so there will be activity here all evening. You shouldn't be too obvious."

"Okay, that'll help," Danny said.

"Also, I told the kitchen staff that you'll be here for several hours, so they'll put out coffee, water, and a few delicacies."

"Oh, you don't have to do that."

Lorenzo smiled. "It's not a problem. Really. We're already set up for the membership meeting, so the coffee is on. And believe me, these guys will never be able to eat all the pastries that Victoria's sends over. So, enjoy. You're helping us out in eliminating any overages."

"Well, thanks. You've been more than generous, and believe me, with this crew, you won't have any leftovers!"

"Good." Lorenzo nodded and smiled. "Well, I'll let you get back to work. I hope you find Lucia."

John knocked on the ground-floor door of what would be a very nice apartment building in any other city, but is only average in North Beach. Liam is standing just behind him.

"Yes?" came a muffled response through the door.

"It's Inspectors John O'Neill and Liam Donnelly, San Francisco Police."

They hold their badges up in front of the peephole. After a few moments, they can hear the sound of locks clicking.

A pretty teenaged girl with a pixie haircut, dressed in sweat-pants and a fleece hoodie, opens the door.

"Hi, Claire," John said. "Thank you for agreeing to talk to us."

"After you called my mom, she said I had to," she replied.

Liam grinned. Claire opens the door wider, and John and Liam file inside and quickly survey the apartment as she closed the door. It is cluttered, but reasonably clean. A glass and brass chandelier lights up a 40-year-old dining room table, obviously an heirloom. A couple of textbooks are opened on the table.

"Sorry to interrupt your homework," Liam said.

Claire shakes her head and shrugs. Liam thinks she's shy, which is curious. It didn't quite line up with the bad girl impression he had gotten from Ann, though he had to admit faulty impressions happen when some people talk with cops.

"You can sit down if you want," Claire said, motioning to the living room.

"Sure," John said. "We won't take much of your time." They each chose a worn chair, while Claire sat down on an equally worn loveseat. "So, you're here alone?"

"Yeah," Claire nodded, her hair bobbing with the movement. "My mom's a nurse at St. Francis Hospital. My dad left when I was little and didn't leave us much. Mom works the swing shift for the extra money."

"So, you're on your own every day after school?" Liam asked.

"Pretty much. Mom leaves a dinner for me, and instructions if she wants me to do anything around the apartment; but usually, I just do my homework and then watch a little TV or something."

John smiled, "Well, you have your priorities straight."

Claire shrugged again, "I want to go to Saint Ignatius with my friends."

"And you have to keep your grades up."

Claire nodded, sending her hair bouncing again. "I don't know if I'll be able to, though."

"Why is that?"

She looked at them as if she were embarrassed. "I guess you heard about my detentions."

"If it makes you feel any better," Liam said, "I went to Catholic school. I seemed to rack up plenty of detentions, myself. Entirely undeserved, I might add, and I still got into Sacred Heart."

Claire smiled and seemed to relax a bit. "Still kept you out of St. Ignatius, though."

"So…" John, an SI grad, suppressed a grin as he winked at Liam. Then he asked, "Is that a regular thing? Friction with the sisters?"

"Only about every week," Claire grumbled, her expression hardening. A bit of fire suddenly appeared behind her eyes.

John raised his eyebrows and nodded, encouraging her to go on. She sighed. "It's usually different things," she grumbled, her voice then shifting to an angry singsong. "I don't

listen well enough to Sister droning on in class, or I'm whis-
pering to my friends, or I'm smoking. Always something."

"What about rolling your skirt?" Liam asked.

Claire's face reddened a bit, but she nodded. "When my
mom wears a skirt, it's not down below her knees. That's
just stupid. So, I roll my skirt a little shorter when I get out
of school." She fumbled nervously with the zipper on her
hoodie. "I like the way men look at me when I pass."

"Why weren't you with Ann and Lucia after detention
yesterday?" John inquired.

Claire rolled her eyes. "I usually roll up my skirt after
turning the corner on Stockton. Somebody saw me and reported me to Sister Mary Joseph. That was my second offense. At least the second one they knew about, and it got
me detention. So, I had to stay for an extra hour."

She shook her head as she sighed, exasperated.

"Do you know where Lucia is?" Liam asked abruptly,
leaning forward.

"No. I know she wasn't at school today, but I didn't know
why. My mom said that she never went home yesterday, and
that you're looking for her."

"And she hasn't contacted you at all?" John asked.

Claire shook her head, her hair swinging back and forth
against her face.

"Do you have any idea where she might have gone?"

"Home?" Claire shrugged. "She wouldn't have run away,
or anything like that. I mean she was pissed about the

detention, but she got along fine with her parents. It's not like she would have been afraid to go home."

John looked over at Liam, disappointment on his face. Liam nodded at him and then turned to Claire. "Well, Claire, I appreciate you taking the time to talk to us." He pulled a card out of his pocket, and John gave her one of his, too. "If you think of anything that might help, or if you hear from Lucia, please give either one of us a call."

"I will," Claire promised, taking the cards.

John stood up. "Okay, we'll let you get back to your homework."

"It's easy," Claire shrugged as if it were no big deal.

"No problems?" Liam asked.

"No." Claire glanced at the books for a moment before looking back at John and Liam. "Just the discipline stuff. If I don't get into Saint Ignatius, it will be because of that, not my grades." Her eyes distorted a little behind the tears forming there. "That will just kill my mom. She's been working so hard to help me."

"I have a feeling you can do it," Liam said with a confident tone.

Claire managed a strained smile and a nod. "I'm going to try."

By 4:00 p.m., plainclothes police officers had spread out across the Washington Square neighborhood. They were talking to everyone — people in the local businesses and at bus stops, churchgoers and priests at Saints Peter and Paul, the nuns, and staff at the grammar school. The Narcotics Squad focused its efforts on the homeless inhabitants of the park.

Shortly thereafter, the Narcotics Supervisor, Sergeant Jim Fornette, punched Lieutenant Lee's number into his phone. Danny answered immediately.

"Lieutenant," Fornette started, "any chance you can find us a Chinese speaker? Mandarin would be preferable, or better yet, one Mandarin and one Cantonese."

"Don't tell me you have a huge Chinese homeless issue out there."

"No, sir. It's just that we're finding the park is really divided into three groups. First, it's the neighborhood folks. We can talk to them, no problem. Then, there's the homeless, and we're making some headway there. Unfortunately, I think some of my guys are relating a little too well. And finally, there are several Chinese people who do their Tai Chi here in the park. We could use some help talking to this group."

"I should have thought of that," Danny replied. "I'll call Central Station and see if they have any Chinese speakers on now. I think the majority here will be speaking Mandarin. I can help a bit, in a pinch, with Cantonese, as my grandparents were from Hong Kong, but my skills are a bit diminished."

"Great. If they find our speakers, have the officers change into soft clothes before coming down."

"Got it."

Fornette watches as his officers speak with different people in the park while showing them Lucia's picture. He sighs as invariably they moved on, shaking their heads.

A few minutes later, his phone rings. It's Lieutenant Lee. "Central is sending over two officers. They can cover both Mandarin and Cantonese."

"Fantastic. Thank you, sir. Can you have them report to you at the Command Post? I'll send one of my people over to get them and brief them on what we're doing."

"Will do, Sergeant. Good catch."

CHAPTER 10

He has already taken care of the van used for the girl. He took it to a car wash and vacuumed it out before washing it inside and out. Then, he dumped the heavy-duty construction bag in a dumpster next to one of a hundred construction sites in Mission Bay. Thinking back to the night before, he is disappointed he didn't get to the special girl, the one with the pixie cut, but in retrospect, her replacement was good, too. He considers his venture a success. The van is now back in the garage.

However, he knows law enforcement technology has changed a lot over the years, sometimes almost daily, requiring his constant adaptation. Used to be, he could grab one of those uppity girls, screw her, and dump her. They never saw his face, never got a look at his vehicle, and he is down the road before they ever started crying to mama.

Now the technology has moved way beyond just gathering and checking fingerprints. They could triangulate the location of a cell phone, collect hair and fiber evidence, DNA samples. And there are fucking cameras everywhere! It is just too risky to leave witnesses any longer.

He was fifteen when he did his first, back in Georgia. Since he was poor, just about any girl was above his station, or at least thought she was. He watches them in the restaurant where he washes dishes for minimum wage. They have the latest fashions, and they only hang out with the rich boys, or the ones who are the star athletes. He dreams about what he would do to one of them if he ever got the chance, but he knows that's not going to happen. He's got no car, no money, no clothes and no chance – he can only dream. Knowing he can't have them and they are way out of his reach, he attacks the only ones who are beneath him – the black girls, of course. It didn't take long before he made that particular discovery; once he knew he could take his pick, grab one, have his way with her, dump her out of the car blindfolded, and move on to the next. She would be too scared or too embarrassed to report it. And if she did, there probably wouldn't be any police manhunt for the suspect. With that knowledge, he began to plan to move on to the 'uppity' girls.

Then came the Army. He had mixed feelings about his time in the service. He liked it well enough, except they valued team players, something he had never been. He liked to think of himself as a lone wolf. Stateside, he would go to bars near the base and drink and watch the girls who were there. He tried to date some of the prettier and classier girls, but they shunned him like he had leprosy. The bar 'hanger-ons' are available, but he isn't interested.

That's not to say he hadn't gotten away with these episodes overseas. He was careful, never leaving behind anything incriminating enough to warrant criminal charges, or a Dishonorable Discharge. A few other guys were not as lucky or careful, and did time in the Army Stockades. For him, the overseas girls were much easier targets.

What distinguishes him is his lone wolf disposition. He tried grabbing girls with a partner once, but that didn't work out. The partner is careless, especially after he starts drinking. Like that old Mafia saying, "Two people can keep a secret, but only if one of them is dead."

That former partner is dangerous, so he too goes missing. He is keeping his secret now.

When he returned stateside, he went back to the local bars. He actually stalked some of the prettier girls until the opportunity presented itself where they were alone and vulnerable. He was always masked, and he always wore gloves. He was never identified even though there were questions about his whereabouts on several occasions when a local girl went missing near a base. All were contributing factors to his Army career lasting only 30 months, and ending with a Less Than Honorable Discharge.

Once he is discharged, he picks up pretty much where he left off in Georgia before the Army. After a while, he starts moving around. As law enforcement technology continues to advance, he has to keep up, enlarging his knowledge base, doing whatever it takes to stay ahead of them. If he is going to survive, he has to be both smart and vigilant.

This became his mantra. Especially after his mistake in Maryland. That bitch had been more resourceful and re-silient than he had counted on. When he took off the re-straints, she kicked him in the balls and hit him with a rock. Then she immediately reported him to the police, describing his van to a T.

He hadn't made it halfway out of town before they pulled him over. She is able to identify him. Plus, her blood is on his clothing and apparently, she had cut herself on the rock, and some of her personal property is still in his van. He does five years in the Maryland State Penitentiary. He makes sure to serve the full five-year sentence, to avoid a parole tail and the monitoring of a parole officer with weekly check-ins and having to get permission to travel. After that, he moved westward — sadder, but definitely wiser.

He puts to use the skills he picked up in the Army. While in maintenance, he learned painting, drywalling, and auto mechanics – all marketable skills as a general handy-man. He is able to change IDs whenever necessary, to work for cash and stay 'under the radar.' He never takes jobs that require a background check or fingerprints. He has several good IDs, and a couple that were more than passable and would work in a pinch. He also owns multiple registrations and plates for his vans, including legitimate ones. Or at least as legitimate as a salvage-swapped vehicle can be. He has worked his way across the country leaving a trail of victims and no viable evidence.

He is ready to go whenever the time comes or he feels threatened. That way of life has served him well. He is ready to leave now, but it won't be right away. He carries a pocketful of cash from the church job, and has over three weeks remaining on his month-to-month rent. He has covered his tracks and will chill for a while before moving on. Fortunately, he isn't like some serial rapists and murderers who need a fix every few days. His needs are infrequent and his lifestyle spartan.

For now, his job is done. He nods approvingly toward the vans and walks into the apartment area. Cleaning up after a rape and murder is dirty work. He goes to the sink to wash his hands. The disinfectant he liked to use burns his hand. He looks down at it and there is a cut on his right hand, on the second knuckle. He doesn't remember hurting it. Maybe it happened when he was finishing up at the church, but no way to know for sure. The gloves he had worn the night before were on their way to a landfill by now.

Still, it is strange. He washed a little more gently around the cut.

CHAPTER 11

By 8:00 p.m., foot traffic in Washington Square had diminished significantly. Most of the businesses are closed, and the church and school are either closed or closing. The park itself is empty except for a few homeless people who haven't yet located a place for the night. The late dinner crowd is arriving at the local restaurants, but chances were slim that any of them would have witnessed something that happened earlier the previous day.

The Supervisors converge on the Command Post to report to Lieutenant Lee. Narcotics is the last to report. "You covered the homeless in the park, right?" Danny asked.

"Yes, sir. The ones still in the park have been interviewed, and we're not seeing any new arrivals. Apparently, the park isn't an ideal overnight location. The parks people water there overnight, so it's uninhabitable. Most of those here now will move on to get a night spot somewhere else."

"Thanks." Danny cocked his head toward the Narcotics Supervisor as a thought occurred to him. "You may have stumbled on to a solution by sending some of our hardcore homeless to a shelter."

"What's the solution?"

"Watering the parks thoroughly at night. You basically flood them and render them uninhabitable. The increased water bill will be more than offset by the eliminating of the cost of the constant homeless sweeps. Who knows?"

He looked at the others crowded into the room around the table. "Let's wrap up and finish back at the Hall of Justice in the Homicide Conference Room. I don't want to overstay our welcome here at the Club; they've been more than gracious. We will debrief there, then you can finish your paperwork and go home."

"What about all those goodies in the kitchen?" one of the Narcotics officers asked. Other heads began nodding, the thought was shared by a number of them.

"If I'm correct, sir, these are for us?" Sergeant Fornette inquired.

Danny answered. "That's right. Grab a couple each."

Fornette then turned to Danny. "There's more here than even this crew can eat. How 'bout we take the rest outside and give them to the homeless people who cooperated with us? After that, if there are any left, we can give them to the shelters we'll pass on the way back to the Hall."

"Great idea," Danny said. "Thanks."

"Well, you know the saying, 'you catch more flies with Italian pastries than with vinegar."

"I'll have Central send over a couple of black and whites," Danny said. "The uniforms can talk to the restaurant crowd, just in case one of them saw anything later in the evening. I know it's a long shot, that the same patron is eating out at the same place two nights in a row, but maybe one of the employees saw something."

He looked down at the coffee cups, napkins, and other trash strewn across the tabletop. "One more thing," he said. "Before we clear out, let's clean up this room, the kitchen, anywhere else we've been tonight. Put our trash in bags and get it outside to a dumpster. I want it to look like we were never here."

"Yes, sir," several said as they all stood up and began gathering the debris.

Danny leaves the room, and following the sound of loud voices, walks to the main hall. The sound is nearly deafening. A large group is gathered there, everyone yelling at once. He sees the club president among them and waves. Lorenzo stands up and comes outside the room, pulling the door closed behind him, muffling the noise slightly.

"Just wanted to thank you," Danny said. "We're clearing out now."

"No problem," Lorenzo replies. "Anything else I can do?"

"No, we're fine." Danny hears the shouting from the main hall now punctuated by a bang, like someone pounding his fist on the top of a table. "What's going on? It sounds like there's about to be a murder in there."

"We're Italian," Lorenzo replies with a laugh, as if that explained it all. "Everyone's shouting, no one's listening, and everyone's happy."

"Phew!" Danny replies with relief.

"By the way," Lorenzo asks, "did you find anything on our little girl?"

"Not sure yet. We're going back to the Hall of Justice now to compare notes and go over all the statements we collected this evening."

"*Buona notte e buona fortuna.* Good night and good luck," Lorenzo said with his hands together, almost as if folded in prayer. "*La velocità di dio.* Go with the speed of God."

Danny having grown up across from North Beach in Chinatown, and knowing a bit of Italian, replies, "*Grazie!*"

CHAPTER 12

Kathy stands outside the interview room at the Hall of Justice, her face registering a sense of urgency as she relates pertinent facts to Raul Hernandez, a Deputy District Attorney. Reggie stands behind her, anxious to get on with the interview.

"His name is William Davis. Fifty-six years old, hardcore, chronic homeless, in and out of the city's Navigation Centers, prefers the street. He doesn't seem to be an alcoholic or under the influence of drugs, and while I'm no expert, his mental health seems about normal. Whatever that is."

"I don't care," Hernandez grouses, shaking his head. "We should have this man evaluated as to his mental capacity, so this interview can stand up at trial."

"I don't think you understand," Reggie says impatiently. "We don't see this guy as the perpetrator. He's a potential witness. We're only going to list him as a person of interest."

"If, during the interview," Kathy added, "we feel he's shifted into the suspect column, we can rethink your mental health evaluation. But right now, time is our worst enemy and we need to get as much information as quickly as possible. Remember, if this is an abduction, and it's looking more and more like it is, we're about out of time."

"Okay," Hernandez said, holding up his hands as if in surrender. "I'm just trying to cover all the bases."

"More like cover his ass and his boss' conviction rate," Reggie mutters under his breath.

"Okay," Kathy says, her voice indicating she is in control. "Let's get started."

She opens the door and they all file in. The interview room is plain and gray, with a table in the middle of the room. An overhead fluorescent light illuminates the homeless man sitting at the table, and the red light on the closed-circuit camera mounted high on the wall indicates he is being recorded.

"Hello, William. I'm Inspector Kathy Sullivan, and these are Inspector Reginald Gibson and Assistant District Attorney Raul Hernandez." William nods to each of them. "Are you feeling okay? Would you like anything to eat or drink?" Kathy continues.

"Somethin' to eat would be much appreciated," William replies, with the familiar whistling S's, "and maybe some coffee. I mean real coffee, not that crap they serve at the shelter."

"How about a burger, with everything," Reggie suggests, "and a Peet's?"

"Oh," William sighs euphorically, "that would be heaven!"

Reggie nods and steps out of the room.

"Now, we need to talk to you about the phone we found in your sleeping bag. But first we'll advise you of your rights." Kathy glances down at the Miranda Card clipped to the folder she held, which also contains the information sheet on William. "You have the right to remain silent. Anything you say can and will be used against you in a court of law. You have the right to have an attorney present during questioning. If you cannot afford an attorney, one will be provided for you."

She looked up at William. "Having heard your rights, do you understand them?"

"Yes."

"Keeping these rights in mind, do you want to talk to us?"

"Sure."

"Do you want to have an attorney present?"

William shakes his head, no. "Never had much use for attorneys." He glances at Hernandez.

"No offense intended. Sure, I'll talk to you, and I don't want no attorney."

Reggie steps back into the room. "Your burger and Peet's coffee are on the way," he says. William unconsciously licks his lips.

"Okay," Kathy says, her tone is 'let's-get-down-to-business'. "First, let's start with where you got the phone. I don't think a pink phone with a Hello Kitty case is exactly you, William."

"No, the phone's not mine," William admits with an embarrassed smile. Then, a thought occurs to him. "Or maybe it is. I found the phone in a trashcan, so the old owner didn't want it anymore, so maybe it is mine. Yeah, I like that. The phone's mine."

"William, I like your logic," Reggie said, "and if you want to say the phone is yours, we can go with that. But what if I tell you the previous owner was murdered, and now you're claiming the dead woman's phone is yours? I think that makes you murder suspect number one."

"Wait," William blurts in a panic, "wait, no, it's not my phone. I didn't murder any woman. I never hurt anyone. I should have left the damn thing in the trash can."

"Okay, William," Kathy says soothingly, "Calm down. Let's go back to the trash can where you found this phone."

She slipped a photo out of the folder and turned it in front of William. It shows Lucia's phone, still contained in the clear plastic evidence bag. "First, is this an accurate photo of the phone you found?"

"Yes, it is," William says, his breathing returning to normal.

"Where exactly did you find the phone?"

"You know Washington Square Park, out in front of the church?" Kathy nods. "Well, there are trash cans all over that park, and compared to a lot of parks in the city, this one has some decent things in the trash."

"All right, you go through the trash cans to see if there's anything worthwhile that you want, is that correct?"

"You got it. So, I'm checking the trash. I ride the bus over there from Mission where I live. Not everyone knows about these trash cans, and the ride's usually worth it."

"Okay, you're going through the trash after you ride the bus over from Mission," Kathy repeats, as William nods in agreement. "Which trash can was the phone in?"

"Well," William starts, closing his eyes, picturing the scene, "when you walk into the park, if your back is toward the church, and you walked straight ahead, you'd see some trash cans over to the right."

"And it was in one of those cans?"

"Yup."

Kathy waits a beat, but he didn't expound. "Which one?"

"Well, there's three cans, and it's in the one on the end closest to the church."

"Thank you." Kathy exhaled, trying not to sound too exasperated. William's a tough interview.

There is a light knock at the door, and Reggie turns to open it and then walks out. He returns after a couple of seconds carrying a cup of Peet's coffee and a large hamburger. William's eyes are nearly the size of the burger as Reggie sets them down in front of him.

Kathy holds up a hand to get his attention away from the food. "One more thing," she says. "Are you willing to take us back to the trash cans and point out which one the phone was in?"

"You bet. Now can I eat?"

"Absolutely. I think we'll all take a break."

Kathy, Reggie, and Hernandez leave William to his re-past and walk back to Homicide, gathering around her desk. They all glance at each other's faces, each trying to read the other's thoughts. Kathy is the first to speak. "I think he's tell-ing the truth, but I want to ask a few more questions. And I think he needs to take us to the trash can so we can see if there's any additional evidence."

"Yeah," Reggie added, "We need patrol to secure those cans right now if we want the contents. I'm afraid they may have been emptied since last night."

"I agree with both of you," Hernandez said. "Let's finish the interview and then go back to the Square to find that can."

Reggie pulls out his phone. "I'll call radio and get patrol to secure those cans."

"Okay," Kathy says, "let's go finish with Mr. Bill."

William is just finishing the last of the burger when they walk in. "Thank you," he says. "That was delicious."

"You're welcome," Kathy replies. "Now, we want to go back to Washington Square, and have you show us exactly which trash can the phone was in."

"Fine with me."

William continues to nurse his cup of coffee as Reggie gathers up the papers from the burger and Kathy takes William's file folder. The butterflies in her stomach remind her they are running out of time.

CHAPTER 13

Lieutenant Lee stands at the head of the table in SFPD Homicide conference room. John, Liam, and the supervisors of the teams who had conducted the interviews in Washington Square are seated around the table. It's been a long day, and most of the supervisors are slouching in their chairs.

"Please tell me we have something to show for this expenditure of money and manpower," Danny says.

"We know that Lucia was at the bakery at 4:00 p.m.," John replies, "and that she turned to the right when she walked out."

"The school confirms she didn't come back onto the school property," Liam added.

Danny nods. "Okay. Narcotics, what did you find out from the homeless people?"

"A few in and around the park say they saw her, or someone that looked just like her, in front of the church at a little after four. This is a little sketchy, since one of the homeless witnesses isn't exactly sure what year it is."

Danny sighs and tips his head toward the Missing Persons Supervisor.

"To add to the confusion," the Supervisor says, "two employees of one of the restaurants on Columbus say a girl that looked like our girl, got on the 30 Stockton bus at about 7:00 p.m., heading downtown."

"The church was open," John noted, "but the local priest said he didn't see anyone inside the church after 4:40 p.m., and definitely no one that looked like our girl."

"What about the third girl?" Danny inquired. "Claire?"

"We met her at their place," Liam said. "She's 14 going on 34. She has a single Mom, a nurse at St. Francis Hospital. Mom works the swing shift for the extra shift differential money, so Claire's on her own after school. She's never been in any real trouble, except for the weekly run-ins with the sisters."

"Overall, she seems like a good girl," John adds. "The nuns have their hands full with her, though."

"Claire said she always rolls up her uniform skirt," Liam continued. "She likes the furtive, admiring looks she gets from the men. She also says she frequently grabs a smoke once they've turned the corner on Stockton. Claire likes Lucia and Ann, even though she thinks they're a little too scared of the good sisters."

John peruses his notes. "We asked her why she wasn't with Lucia and Ann after detention yesterday, and she informed us since this is her second so-called conviction, she had to do extra detention… she didn't get out for another hour."

"In spite of her rather hard exterior," Liam says, "she's well aware that her mom is working hard to pay the tuition. She wants to go to Saint Ignatius with Ann and Lucia, and knows she has to clean up her act this semester. I don't think the Jesuits will be quite as gullible as the good sisters. She'll definitely need some financial aid to cover SI tuition, but I think she can make it."

"Yeah, she's evidently got the grades," John said, wrapping it up, "but she knows the discipline issue will hurt her. So, she's going to try. We'll see."

"And no information about Lucia?" Danny asked.

"Afraid not."

"So," Danny recounts, "bakery at four, confirmed. Not in the church, confirmed, and Claire says Lucia was gone when she got out of detention. Finally, maybe outside the church and maybe on the bus, both up in the air."

"That about sums it up," Liam nodded.

"Great." Danny is definitely less than pleased.

CHAPTER 14

The streetlights are on when the car pulls up to Washington Square, but the park remains quite dark beneath the old-growth trees. Still, the area is busy with diners crossing after exiting Original Joe's, North Beach Restaurant, and others in the area. Kathy, Reggie, Hernandez, and William, the homeless man, pile out of the car. In the partial light, they see patrol officers watching over several trashcans.

"So," Kathy asks, "which trashcan is the one?"

"It's the one next to the bus stop," William replies.

"The stop on Columbus?" Reggie asks.

"Yeah, where the number 30 bus stops."

As they make their way to the trashcans it's not obvious if the trash has been collected. Reggie takes out his phone and calls Public Works. After two rings, the call is answered. "This is Inspector Reggie Gibson, SFPD. I need trash can liner pick-ups for the cans at Washington Square, and replacement liners dropped off so the cans can still be used."

The man at Public Works responded in a loud voice. Reggie held the phone away from his ear. "Are you kidding?" the man asked. "What are we supposed to do with, what is it, eight full trashcan liners?"

"My partner and I will be waiting here for you. We'll mark each liner by location, while you replace them with new, empty liners. Then, we'll follow the truck back to the Hall of Justice where we'll relieve you of the trash."

"You got it, Inspector," the man concedes, "but you'll have to admit, even by San Francisco standards, this is weird."

"No argument here," Reggie replies. "Thanks."

As William waits in the car; Kathy, Reggie, and Hernandez watch the Public Works crew pick up the trashcan liners. They are marked according to their location in the park and loaded on the truck. The eighth bag, the one by the bus stop, is put in the trunk of their car.

Once the liners are delivered to the Hall of Justice, the first seven bags are tagged as evidence. They are placed in a secure storage bin that opens to the outside, so as to not overwhelm the evidence room staff with the pungent smell of garbage.

Kathy looks down at the garbage from the eighth bag, which has been spread out on a large sheet of paper on the floor in the evidence room. She shakes her head as she turns to Hernandez. "Well," she says, "we have the proverbial good news and bad news. The good news being there is almost nothing in this trash liner. The bad news is the garbage was picked up since our guy found the phone. So, in all likelihood, this little bit of garbage is useless. Still, we'll have William look at it in the morning to confirm."

"So, that's it for the garbage patrol?" Hernandez asked.

"No, we'll go through all of the liners in the morning to be sure, and we'll confirm the pickup schedule with the trash folks." She looked back down at the trash on the floor and sighs. "But I think we're out of luck with this stuff." She turned back to Hernandez. "Oh, by the way, thanks for hanging out to see this through. I take back all the bad things I've said about the prima donnas in the DA's office."

"*No es nada,*" Hernandez smiled. "What are you planning to do with Mr. Bill?"

"Great question. I don't think given the trash can scenario, we could ever get a possession of stolen property charge to stick, right?"

"Absolutely. They'd laugh me out of the office. However, given that he's going to assist you in the morning, and since he may have knowledge critical to this case, you can hold him as a Material Witness. I don't think you'll get any objections from Mr. Bill, given a warm bed and a couple of meals."

"Thanks, that's perfect. So, that's it for the trash for now. Let's go see what Reggie has." As Reggie finishes with William in the interview room, Kathy and Hernandez enter.

"William, we need you to take a look at the contents of the trash liner, if you don't mind," Kathy says. "That'll be in the morning, though, so we're going to hold you overnight as a Material Witness."

William's face screws up in puzzlement. "What does that mean?"

"Basically, room and board," Hernandez answers, "until tomorrow when you take a look at the trash liner."

"Sounds good to me, but what about my stuff on Mission Street?"

"We'll have someone keep an eye on your stuff overnight."

They walk upstairs to the jail floor. Kathy tells the custody officer to place William in a cell by himself as a Material Witness, give him another meal, and they will come and collect him in the morning. Hernandez leaves as Reggie and Kathy head to the Homicide Conference Room.

CHAPTER 15

John, Liam, and a few others are in the Conference Room when Kathy and Reggie enter.

"We're just getting up to speed on our interviews from the Square tonight," Danny says. "What can you add to this mystery?"

"We've got William, our homeless fellow," Reggie replied, "in a cell for the night as a Material Witness, with ADA Hernandez' approval. We don't think he's got anything to do with the missing girl other than finding the phone. We collected the trash liners from the cans in the park where he found the phone, but don't hold your breath. It looks like the trash was picked up between the phone toss and our getting there."

"Where are we on the GPS?"

"Our IT people are willing to work all night," Kathy replies, "but evidently the private sector doesn't work the midnight shift. AT&T promised a full review of the GPS by 9:00 a.m. tomorrow."

"Okay," Danny sighed. "Tomorrow the shit will hit the fan. The press will be all over this. The Archbishop will be all over the Chief, the Chief will be all over me, and as a result, I'll be all over you. So, let's try and get ahead of the curve, even if it's just one step ahead."

"Kathy and Reggie, since you both live in town, you get in early, say 7:00 in the morning. John and Liam, since you have the longer commute, you come in at about noon and plan on staying late. Let's all plan on some long hours for the next several days. And Kathy, start calling AT&T about that GPS information as soon as you get in."

"Yes, sir."

Alright. Good work today. Get some rest." With that, Danny leaves the Conference Room.

"Well," John says, "since I have the longest drive, and I've got options, why don't I drop off Reggie? Kathy, you can drop Liam off before going over the hill to your place."

"Works for me."

Less than five minutes later, they separate in the garage walking toward their respective cars.

"Since I have the early shift tomorrow," Kathy says to Liam, "I'll drop you off, head home, and get some sleep and pack a go bag, just in case this involves staying later than any of us planned on. Plus, I'll have to pick up Reggie in the morning."

"Yeah," Liam sighs, "that sounds like the logical thing to do. Dammit."

Kathy glanced at Liam to find him appreciatively looking her up and down. She smiles.

Papers are strewn across the conference table early the next morning as Kathy, Reggie, and Lieutenant Lee peruse all the reports submitted the night before by the officers conducting the interviews in Washington Square.

"There's one," Reggie said, "and I repeat, only one potential witness who says Lucia got on the 30 Stockton bus going toward downtown. Even so, we need to get a list of the drivers from Muni who were on the number 30 the previous afternoon and evening, and show them her picture."

"Let's add that to our To Do list," Danny says.

Kathy is quiet, pondering the next steps. "Lieutenant," she finally says, "do you think we should organize a task force for this operation and get ahead of the press and the powers that be? This is going to take significant manpower, and we just don't have the numbers here in Homicide."

"That's a good idea," Danny says. "I'll set up the framework and we can put together a list of 'next steps'. Then I'll hit up the Chief for the extra personnel."

They continue sifting through the reports until the silence is punctuated by the electronic tone of the phone. Reggie, the closest one to it, picked it up. "Homicide. Hold on." He holds the receiver out toward Kathy. "For you."

"Inspector Sullivan," she listened for a few moments. Her face progressively brighter. "Excellent! Can you email the spreadsheet to me at the department? Thank you so much."

She hands the receiver back to Reggie, who hangs it up. "That was AT&T. They have the GPS information on Lucia's phone and they're sending it right now. I'll go out to my desk and download the sheet and make copies. Be right back."

She is back within a few minutes, looking at the sheet as she comes in the door.

"Look at this. Lucia is at Victoria's from 3:55 to 4:05. That confirms the counter person's recollection. Lucia leaves and walks past the front of the church. She must stop there since there isn't any movement for almost ten minutes."

"Eating the cannoli, no doubt," Reggie says.

"Right," Danny adds. "Where to from there?"

"She walks across the street to the park, and then crosses back."

"To put the wrapper in the trash," Reggie interprets again.

"She walks to Stockton and turns for home. She gets about half a block and stops again. She's there for almost five minutes. Then she moves along Stockton again."

"Okay, mystery number one," Danny says, "why the stop?"

Kathy ignores the question as she continues looking at the data. "Well, this can't be right. The GPS shows another stop in the Presidio, almost to the Golden Gate, in what looks like a parking lot next to one of the old Fort Baker batteries. The problem is there's only a 20-minute time lapse. No way she could walk that fast."

"So, she is picked up," Reggie said. "But by whom… and why?"

"It looks like she moves from the parking area to one of the old gun batteries. She's there for more than 30 minutes, then back to the parking area." Kathy scans further down the sheet. "Now she's all over the place, too fast to be walking, must be driving and in circles. It looks like she stops again, out off of 33rd Ave, next to the Legion of Honor."

"What time is it now on the GPS?" Reggie asks.

"7:30 p.m."

He shakes his head. "It's dark and the Museum has been closed for an hour and a half. Now the GPS says she's going toward the tenth green at the Lincoln Park Golf Course, walking this time."

"The 10th at Lincoln is right next to the Legion of Honor," Danny says.

"She's there for another 15 minutes, and then on the move again."

"I don't like the way this is playing out," Danny says, his forehead wrinkled with worry.

"Where is she heading now?"

"Directly back to Washington Square," Kathy replies, puzzled, "and to the Columbus Avenue side."

"The trash can," Reggie says.

"GPS is stationary for an hour, then it's traveling again on Columbus. It ends up at 8th and Mission, where it is still pinging when the police arrived. Evidently found its way to Mission after William had done his dumpster dive for the phone."

"I'm sending Johnston and Dominguez out to the Presidio with a CSI Team to see if there's any physical evidence to be found. Kathy, give them the GPS coordinates so they're not wandering all over hell's half acre."

Liam decides now is the time to add his two cents. "Lieutenant, I think the Presidio is the U.S. Park Police's jurisdiction, and they might get a little bent out of shape if we just charge in."

Danny thinks for a moment before responding. "My initial response? Who cares? This case is a priority, and I want our evidence people handling the scene... but you're right. It's their turf, so a heads-up is in order."

Reggie has already Googled the Presidio and sent the information to Lt. Lee's computer. With the Inspectors gathered by his desk, Danny begins to read the Presidio history out loud to the assembly: "The Presidio of San Francisco exists completely within the confines of the City and County of San Francisco. It has a rich history and is now an entity unto itself. The Presidio (originally, El Presidio Real de San Francisco or The Royal Fortress of Saint Francis) is a park and former U.S. Army military fort on the northern tip of the San Francisco Peninsula in San Francisco, California, and is part of the Golden Gate National Recreation Area.

It is one of the most beautiful pieces of land in the Bay Area. It's over 1,500 acres of historic buildings, weapons, and armaments evolving from smooth bore cannons to modern missiles, a golf course, an airstrip, and a cemetery. That cemetery is the oldest national cemetery on the West Coast, and the final resting place of many Medal of Honor awardees, and it's also the home of some of the most breathtaking views imaginable of the Bay and the Pacific Ocean. It's evolved from a military base to a National Recreation Area, and now to include the Bay Area homes of Disney and Lucas Films.

Historically, from 1776 to 1821, the Presidio is the Spanish empire's northernmost military outpost and guarded California's largest harbor from occupation by other European powers including Russia and Britain.

In 1821, Mexico declared its independence from Spain. There was no change in personnel when the Presidio changed from Spanish to Mexican sovereignty.

In 1848, after the end of the Mexican-American War, this large military reservation at the Golden Gate developed into the most important Army post on the Pacific Coast. Over time it became the nerve center of a coastal defense system that eventually included Alcatraz and Angel Island.

From 1848 to about 1890, the Presidio defended San Francisco and also participated in the Indian Wars in the West. From 1898 to 1973, the Presidio was a key link in the projection of American military power into the Pacific Basin, and further west onto the mainland of Asia.

In 1994 it became part of the Golden Gate National Recreation Area and came under the jurisdiction of the U.S.

Park Police. There would be no commercial or residential development. Real estate agents, brokers and developers were lining up to jump from the Golden Gate Bridge. But it was the right decision."

"That is actually pretty interesting," Kathy said. "I've lived here all my life and I didn't know half of that."

"Okay," Danny continues. "Kathy and Reggie, you drive out to the tenth green at Lincoln Park and see what you can find. Harry and Chris, get with CSI and go to the Presidio. Hold there and call the Park Police to meet you. Explain you just want them to stand by while you look for any possible evidence; they won't have to take any paper. Call me immediately on the phone, no radio, if you find anything, or if there are any issues." He takes a deep breath as he stands and takes his jacket from the back of the chair. "I'll go and brief the Chief."

Soon, Danny is sitting in front of the Chief's desk, completing his briefing on their findings from the last 24 hours.

"So," Chief Walker begins, "I gather what you're preparing me for is the worst-case scenario of a body being recovered at Lincoln Park."

"I'm afraid so," Danny replied. "That GPS pattern suggests an abduction, or maybe, hopefully, she has a boyfriend with a car, and they ran away. She could have dumped the phone when she realized it had the GPS feature."

"Tell me you actually believe that last part."

Danny sighs. "No, I'm afraid I don't. But I'm sure as hell holding out hope that it's true. Mom and Dad can probably live with a teenage indiscretion, but the other will kill them…"

Danny's phone interrupted his comments. It's Harry. Danny explains to the Chief he needs to take the call. The Chief motions his approval.

When Danny picks up, Harry explains that the Park Police, after hearing the news teases, are asserting jurisdiction and demanding that the SFPD withdraw. Danny gathers himself; rather than instigate an interjurisdictional dispute, he takes a breath, and tells Harry to have everyone standby and he will call back.

The Chief leans forward with his elbows on his desk, his hands clasped tightly. "What's wrong?"

After pausing a beat, Danny explains the jurisdictional issue facing the Inspectors and CSI at the Presidio.

The Chief didn't bother pausing before he responded. "What the fuck is wrong with those clowns? The Missing Persons report, and any related possible crimes are always the responsibility of the lead agency taking the report." He picks up his phone and requests that his assistant get ADA Hernandez on the line.

After just a brief hold, Hernandez picks up. "What can I do for you, Chief?"

"You can get the Park Police at the Presidio, the hell out of my officers' way and let them do their job."

"Chief, is this about the missing girl?"

"You're damned right it is."

"Chief, there's a problem. That's Federal jurisdiction, I don't have any juice."

"Call someone at the U. S. Attorney's Office, and get them to move Smokey the Bear the fuck out of our way."

Hernandez decides this isn't the time to point out that Smokey the Bear is actually Smokey Bear, and he belonged to the Division of Forestry, not the Park Police. Maybe Ranger Rick would have been more appropriate, but given the Chief's state of mind, discretion is the better part of valor.

"Chief, I've got a law school buddy in the U.S. Attorney's Office. Let me make a call."

"Make it fast!"

The Chief hung up, sat back down, and looked at Danny. "If the abduction scenario plays out and we're faced with a possible homicide, are you prepared to deal with the circus that will follow?"

"I think we should immediately set up a Missing Person task force to look for Lucia. That will put us ahead of the curve if this goes bad. Then we can just reconstitute the task force as a Homicide task force, and show we're on top of a rapidly developing set of circumstances."

"Good idea." The Chief sits back, the worry creasing across his face. "God, I hate having to play politics with this little girl's life." He sighs heavily. "Okay, what do you need?"

"People. Can I draw from a couple of the other Bureaus? I'm thinking about 20 total."

"Consider it done. Implement the Missing Persons task force and let me know immediately if anything changes."

The phone rings again. The Chief picks it up. It's Hernandez. "OK, I talked to my buddy, and he understands the gravity of the situation. He's calling the Park Police Major, and in about two minutes the Park Police officers will be standing down and offering their full cooperation."

"Great." As a seasoned veteran of several political wars, and a pragmatist, the Chief knows what to ask next: "What's this cost me?"

Hernandez laughs. "Just mention the valuable cooperation and assistance of both the Park Police and the U. S. Attorney's Office, especially assistant U. S. Attorney Tony Estrada."

The Chief pauses before replying, "Can do, and thank you for straightening this out and eliminating a jurisdictional war that no one would win."

"You're welcome."

Danny immediately calls Harry with the news.

While the jurisdictional lines were being drawn and re-drawn at the Hall of Justice, the suspect is planning his departure.

He sits in his small living area watching the news on his little portable TV. The missing girl is still the lead story, but so far, she is only considered missing. Sooner or later, she will be the murdered, missing girl, and the pressure on the police will be ramped up. But for now, he has a brief respite. The question is what to do with this down time. He gets up and walks to his two vans. This might just be the time to get rid of one and begin preparations for his road trip. Both vans are almost identical, but one is clearly a better mechanical bet. His murder van will be the keeper, for all the right reasons… mechanical and sentimental.

He goes to the painting van and begins to remove all the painting equipment. It takes him more than an hour to have the van completely cleaned out and stripped of any remaining items that might lead the police to him. He stacks the painting supplies in the corner, as they would eventually accompany him when he moved to his next location. The 'I'm a freelance, self-employed, painter' cover story is perfect. It justified the van, it allows him to negotiate for cash payments, and because he is good, there are no questions asked. He still has IDs to spare and with the vans cleaned out, it is time to finish and wash them both.

The painting van will be first. He climbs in and drives to 10th and Harrison to the self-service car wash. He first scrubs the exterior, then he opens all the doors, places plastic bags over the front seats, and power washes the interior. Once the van is clean, he drives back to his place and switches to the murder van. Then back to the car wash. Once both vans are cleaned to his exacting standards, he lets them dry in the garage. He takes the registration and 'pink slip' to the painting van and held it up to the light. It is very good, probably will even fool a dealer, but it didn't have to. He knows it's more than sufficient for a hand-to-hand private party sale. He calls the San Francisco Muni Railway and confirms the busses, and or streetcars, that would be involved in getting him from his place to the Home Depot store in Daly City.

Placing the registration and 'pink slip' in his pocket, and a For Sale sign on the front seat, he drives to the Home Depot store, via Starbucks. The store is a gathering place for workers trying to get cash, day jobs. Many can improve their chances of employment if only they had a vehicle, and a van is one of the vehicles most desired. At the Home Depot he sees no fewer than 20 men vying for customers' attention. He backs into a parking space where the van will face the men. He places the For Sale sign in the front window. Then he opened the driver's door, takes the lid from his coffee, drinks, and waits.

His plan works just as he expected. Within the first half hour he has four inquiries and two seem serious. He tells the most serious pair that the first ones who get back with the $1,000, are the new owners. After an hour and four more nibbles later, one of the serious buyers returns with the cash. The transaction takes only 20 minutes, and he is on the bus heading for home. The van is long gone, and he has a cash infusion for his pending departure.

CHAPTER 16

Liam and John are poring over the papers on the Conference Room table, familiarizing themselves with all the information gathered in the last 24 hours. Their perusal is disturbed when a group of ten file into the room.

"Can I help you?" Liam asked.

"We were told to report here to Lieutenant Lee," one replies. "He's in his office, on the phone. Are you here to join the task force?"

"That's right," the leader of the group responds. In support of his answer, the rest of them nod.

"Well, in that case, welcome and pull up a seat. We'll bring you up to speed."

Reggie buckled his seat belt as Kathy pulled away from the Pro Shop at Lincoln Park Golf Course. "That was nice," he said. "The Starter offered the help of their maintenance department. I told him it's not necessary. We're just looking for some evidence."

"I hope that's all it is," Kathy replies. Reggie can hear the tightness in her voice. A minute later, she pulls into a parking space in the lot at the Legion of Honor. "You play golf?" Reggie asks as they got out of the car.

"I tried it a few times."

"Tried?"

"I decided there were plenty of other things that could goad me to such a level of frustration without having to pay for it!"

Reggie smiles. "I hear you. Well, the tenth hole here at Lincoln comes up to a green situated on a small plateau. When you putt out, you walk off to the eleventh tee over there." Kathy looks in the direction he pointed, only mildly interested. "Lincoln has a number of trees and shrubs all over the course. It's pretty lush for a Muni course."

"Muni course?"

"Municipal. It's owned and operated by the city, as opposed to a private club."

"Oh, of course. So, what about this tenth green area?"

"Lots of greenery to the left of the green and around to the eleventh tee. I've played here, so maybe we'll find a few of my lost golf balls. We should start there."

They split up and started searching the grounds, looking at the grass for clues, and poking through bushes. It didn't take long.

"Kathy, over here." She doesn't like the tone of Reggie's voice.

"Nooo," she replies, her voice a quiet groan.

Reggie breathes out. "Yes… a young girl. She's partially in and actually half out of a garbage bag; she's dead. It looks like there's clothing too. There's a uniform skirt protruding from under her, and what looks like a torn white blouse." He straightens up and looks at Kathy. "Based on the school photo, it's definitely Lucia."

"Fuck!" Kathy put her hand over her eyes for a moment. Then she looks back at Reggie.

"Excuse me. I was just hoping this would turn out differently."

"I know. Why don't you let the Lieutenant know, and he can send the necessary people. We'll have to wait for the Coroner and Forensics, so I'm going to cover her."

"Are you sure? What about disturbing the body? You know, evidence and all that stuff."

"Fuck 'em," Reggie shakes his head as he takes off his jacket. "If it were my daughter, I'd want her covered."

"Roger that," Kathy replies, trying to regain her professional stoicism. "I'll call the Lieutenant."

"Shit, shit, shit!" Danny blew out a sharp breath. "Are you sure? No chance it's not her?"

"It's her, Lieutenant. We're going to start looking around the area, but we're going to need some help and some protection from above."

"I know. I'll notify the Coroner and the Forensics people, and they'll respond incognito.

What else do you need?"

"I appreciate your help from the departmental above, but we actually need protection from above. I'm talking about the press and drones."

Danny pauses just a second. "I'll have the Forensics people bring one of those pop-up tent things that will shield the scene from prying eyes."

"Thanks LT. We'll need some bodies to conduct a top-to-bottom search of this whole area and to keep the press folks off our backs. Someone to tell the Starter at Lincoln the tenth and eleventh are closed for repairs. We'll need to cordon off part of the parking lot at The Legion of Honor for our responding vehicles so we can get set up."

"Okay, you got it. We've just established the Missing Persons task force, and I have ten members plus John and Liam on their way to you, as we speak. We'll have ten more shortly. The departmental PIO will handle the press, and I'll have Richmond Station handle Lincoln and the Legion. I'm on my way to the Chief's office, then I'll try and get out there. If you need anything, and I mean anything, call. I'll take any calls from you, no matter where I am."

"Thank you, Lieutenant. I know this one's a bitch."

"It is, but we do what we have to do. And at least I can say with every confidence that I've got my best people on it."

After Kathy hung up, Danny turned to the Chief. "It's definitely her?" Chief Walker just put his head in his hands.

"You're sure."

"I'm afraid so, sir."

"What do you need me to do?"

"Well, the press is going to be all over this. We'll need our PIO people to be up to speed before they take on the media. This will probably go national, given that her dad's a firefighter."

"Okay. Where do you want them, and when?"

"I'm thinking as soon as I leave your office, and in the Conference Room in Homicide."

"Okay, what else?"

"Given that this whole thing appears to have started at the church, the press will no doubt try to draw some preconceived conclusion that the responsible party is a pedophile priest. So, I think the Archbishop needs to be prepared, and the school and church had better be ready for the onslaught. I think the Archdiocese should have their own PIO ready to intercept the press and they have to be in contact with our press people. We should probably have some officers from Juvenile go out to the school to protect the kids from the media."

"Done. I'll have the Deputy Chiefs here for an update once you've met with your people." The tone of finality in the Chief's voice and his hand reaching for the phone, tells Danny the meeting is over.

He stands up and heads back to Homicide.

CHAPTER 17

The Chief's office is crowded as Danny briefs the Deputy Chiefs on the status of the investigation of Lucia's abduction and murder.

"We have a homeless man in our custody," Danny says, "picked up last night, and he's being held as a Material Witness. Without casting aspersions on the media, I'm betting he'll be a person of interest within a few hours.

"I'm having some of my people go to the family and prepare them for what may transpire." As almost an afterthought, Danny turns to the Chief. "Can we have that priest from the Chaplain's Office meet us there to be of assistance?"

"Absolutely."

"The task force will be out, all hands on deck, in a few hours," Danny continues. "They'll be talking to every business, every person on the sidewalk, bus driver, cabbie, and anyone else who might have been in the area and could have seen anything. We'll be in a race with the press to get to these potential witnesses."

"We'll add personnel at Central," said the Patrol Deputy Chief. "We'll flood the area with black and whites as well."

"Great, thanks." Danny nodded. "I'm going to have my people and the task force people work with the forensics teams to check every stop that showed on that GPS spread sheet. Maybe someone saw something. Or someone."

"Let me know when your Inspectors are going to head over to see the family," the Chief said. "I'll have the Chaplain meet with them."

Danny nods and turned back to the Deputy Chiefs. "I know I'm not telling you anything you don't already know, but I think I can anticipate some of the questions that will be asked. Here are some of the answers."

He looks down at the list in his hand. "Why did you wait a day to look for this girl? We didn't. The patrol officers initiated a search and a door-to-door canvass immediately."

"Why did you wait to create a task force? We began to investigate with our standard resources. We were hoping this was a simple case of a teenager overreacting to a school incident and that she would be home in a few hours."

"Why did you arrest the homeless man? Is he illegal? No arrests have been made. No persons, legal or illegal, have been arrested. One man is currently assisting us as a material witness."

"Is there a task force at this time? Yes, the Missing Persons task force, which was created as soon as we discovered the victim's phone, and has since been reconstituted as a potential Homicide task force. We'll know more as soon as we have a cause of death."

"Are you looking at the Archdiocese' list of pedophile priests as possible suspects? We do not have a suspect at this time. Throughout the investigation, we will look at anyone who could be a potential suspect."

"There may be more, but those are the ones who came to mind immediately."

"Okay," the Chief brings the briefing to a close. "I'll give those questions to the PIO, and I'll send her down to your office to be briefed." Danny nodded his agreement. "Alright, let's get out there and find whoever did this."

Evidence markers dot the ground in the area where Lucia's body was found. Investigators swarmed over the green and the parking lot, and every place in between, looking for any trace of evidence that might point them to the perpetrator.

Kathy stands apart from them, her phone pressed to her ear. "Has everyone arrived?" Danny asks.

"Yes. Liam, John, and the task force are here, as well as Forensics. The Coroner just got here and he's saying, off the record, strangulation, and potential sexual assault. Forensics is about to do their thing and we're talking to anyone who will listen."

"One more thing," Danny said hesitantly. "Someone is going to have to tell the family what we have. Can you and Reggie break free and meet the Chaplain to deliver the news?"

"Sure," Kathy replied sadly. "It makes sense. We were there before and they're familiar with us. Let me see if the coroner will clean up her face so we can take a Polaroid that doesn't look like an autopsy photo."

"Bring a photo of the phone for confirmation, too."

"Will do. We'll leave John and Liam in charge and head to the family residence. Can you give me the contact information for the Chaplain so we can meet ahead of time?"

"Done. Thank you."

Mr. Rosini's face darkened when he opened the door. When he saw the Chaplain standing there with Kathy and Reggie, he knew something was horribly wrong.

"Come in," he says quietly, and opens the door wider. Then as he closed the door behind them, he looks at the three of them. "Tell me why you're here before my wife gets here. I need to be prepared."

"We're pretty sure this will be bad news," Kathy says, her voice unnaturally level, concentrating on her tone. "We want you to look at photos of a phone, and of a girl we found."

"If you think this could be Lucia," Reggie said, "a formal ID would have to take place later today. So, how do you want to handle this? Do you want to look at the photos first, or wait for your wife?"

"I'll do it," Mr. Rosini said. "Then I can tell her without her having to see the photos. Is it bad?"

"If it's your daughter," Kathy replied, "it will be bad. If you mean, is it difficult to look at, then the answer is no."

Mr. Rosini takes a deep breath and lets it out slowly. "Okay, show me."

Kathy hands him the photo of the phone in the pink Hello Kitty case. The photo shook in his hand as he looked at it and nods, his breaths coming faster.

"That looks like her phone," he whispered.

Kathy took a deep breath herself and shows him the photo of the girl's face. Mr. Rosini begins sobbing immediately. The priest steps forward and puts his arm around Rosini's shoulders, helping to support him.

After a few moments, Mr. Rosini is able to nod his head. "It's her."

"No!"

Everyone looked up. They hadn't seen Mrs. Rosini standing there, watching the proceedings.

"No, no, no!" she repeats, her voice rising. Mr. Rosini pulled away from the priest and went to his wife, holding her tightly as she cries into his chest.

A few minutes later, Kathy and Reggie sit for a moment in the car, their shoulders and bodies visibly sagging. Reggie rubs his hands over his head, as if trying to scrub the scene in the Rosini's home from his memory.

"God," he sighs, "I'll never get used to these notifications, no matter how many we do."

"I know." Kathy's tone retained the neutral level required for any semblance of concentration. "It just rips your heart out. I can't imagine losing a child."

She put the key in the ignition and turned it, glad to have an activity to focus on. "What did the Chaplain say?" she asks.

"That he'll bring Mr. Rosini to the Coroner's office for the formal ID. It'll be a little later, though. He said he'd call when they were on their way."

"Good," she replies, and puts the car in gear.

"I'm glad the Chaplain was here," Reggie said quietly. "I think it made an impossibly difficult situation a little easier for the family." He sighs again, "And for us."

CHAPTER 18

Police Department's PIO briefed the assembled media on the discovery of a young girl's body on the Lincoln Park Golf Course. The PIO states that the body has been positively identified as 14-year-old Lucia Rosini. The Press Officer then answers the previously anticipated questions and explains the existence of a newly, reconstituted, Homicide Task Force to address the crime.

"Will the FBI be involved in this case?" a reporter asks.

"As of now, this case hasn't crossed over the jurisdictional lines that would dictate the involvement of the FBI. However, the SFPD is most certainly not averse to asking for the assistance of any agency that could lend a hand."

The press conference ends. It had been attended by all the news stations and become the lead story, every hour on the hour, for KCBS, San Francisco's 24-hour news radio station.

In the apartment area of his 'hide-out', the suspect is organizing his thoughts in order to formulate the perfect exit strategy. As he planned, he listened to the radio.

The lead story told of the discovery of the body, and the case changing from a missing person to a homicide investigation. No real news there. He fully expected the police to discover the body. He is covered — there isn't any physical evidence, and certainly no witnesses. As the story unfolded, there is talk of bringing in the FBI.

"What the fuck…"

He knows enough to know the FBI doesn't have any jurisdiction in a local homicide case… unless the SFPD invites them in. And that might involve admitting the case is above the SFPD's abilities… not likely. The reporter goes on to explain the young victim is the daughter of a 'hero' San Francisco Firefighter and a beloved member of the Catholic, Italian American community in North Beach.

"Shit."

There is no way he could have known about her father's standing and the neighborhood. With the Police and Fire connection, and the press coverage, the FBI's involvement is inevitable. Too much attention, too much pressure.

The clock is ticking.

Liam sits at his desk, looking over the timeline on the Rosini case and already dreading the upcoming funeral. Kathy and Reggie are just back from their horrible day of discovering Lucia's body and notifying the family. John is in the Lieutenant's office, discussing the possibility of additional people to work the funeral. It is getting close to normal quitting time and they were all drained.

John returns to his desk as Lieutenant Lee walks over to the four inspectors. "Go home. Today was a bitch, and tomorrow will be worse. You're no good to me, or the case, if you're out on your feet."

They begin the process of clearing their desks and taking home whatever paperwork they deemed necessary, despite the Lieutenant's instructions. Liam walks over to Kathy's desk.

"How 'bout since you had such a shitty day, I send John home, then I can ride with you and Reggie while you drop him off, and then I'll buy you dinner?"

Kathy puts down her paperwork and turns to face him. "Thank you. I accept and appreciate your most gracious offer. And it's a really nice offer."

Liam tells John about the change in normal plans. "You don't have to tell me twice," he said. "A shortened commute and an early out. All I need is Susan to meet me at the front door with a cocktail and it's the trifecta."

Kathy alerts Reggie there would be three along for the ride to Reggie's place as the four inspectors take the elevator to the garage. John tells Liam he would see him in the morning, and then backed out of his parking space. He pulls out of the Hall of Justice and heads for home, followed by the other three in the second car.

The ride from the Hall of Justice is unusually silent without Liam. Both Inspectors, with years of experience and numerous investigations under their belts, are already worn out.

Certain cases have a way of reaching out and grabbing you. In this case, there are so many elements that made it special.

He drives up 9th Street, across Market and down Larkin Street to Sutter. Sutter to Franklin, then down Franklin to Bay. Finally, he turns on Bay toward the Golden Gate Bridge. Most people would have turned left on Lombard and taken Lombard all the way to the Bridge approach, but a smart cop like John knew Lombard had a traffic signal every other block. But once Bay turns into Marina, there is nothing but clear sailing.

He turned off the AM radio and heard the police band in the background. As he went through the new Doyle Drive Tunnels and onto the approach to the Bridge, he took the last Presidio exit and drove down to Crissy Field. He didn't want to go home just yet.

He parks overlooking the Bay and the bridge, turns off the car and sits. He knows if he goes straight home, his mood will be contagious, and he'll spoil the evenings of three other people. He needs a few minutes to just think.

This case is horrible in so many ways. The victim could have been his daughter, close to the same age, her whole life in front of her, a good kid… and for no reason. He thinks about the Rosini family, and again thinks of his own. How his dad was a native San Franciscan, a civil servant, a police officer, and his mom worked to help make ends meet. Those civil servant police officer salaries weren't all they were cracked up to be.

How? Why? There just aren't any easy answers.

He puts the car in gear and drives to the old gun emplacements and the tunnel where Lucia was murdered. Once again, he parks, only this time he gets out and walks around the lot and into the tunnel. Even though it is just dusk, the tunnel is dark... the last sights Lucia would have seen. A dark, damp, lonely, tunnel; helpless and at the mercy of a total stranger who turns out to be a psychopathic killer. There was a hood in the bag. Was she wearing it? Or did she see the water? The ocean would have looked dark and foreboding, endless, hopeless. Maybe the hood was still on. Maybe she never saw the water.

John finds himself torn between rage and an overwhelming sense of sorrow and helplessness. Even if they solve the case tomorrow, the damage is done, and a family has been destroyed. He wanted to scream. Instead, he walks back to his car, sits down, and calls home. He tells Susan that he will be late and she and the kids should go ahead and eat without him. Not an unusual occurrence by any means, but John's tone tells her something isn't right. She asks if there was anything she could do; John replies it is just a difficult case. She asks if he wants to talk.

"Yes," he says. He knows that is the reason he called in the first place. Susan is smart and knows him better than anyone. She tells him to take his time and she will be waiting when he gets home.

John hesitates a moment and then adds, "Thanks Suz, you always know exactly what to say. I love you."

"I love you, too. Be careful and I'll be waiting."

John hangs up. He feels a bit better. Susan has that effect on him. She is his partner, Father Confessor, confidant, and best friend. She will listen and then carefully point him in the right direction.

He sits for a while longer, remembering back to his years at St. Ignatius High School, when he and some friends would come to the very same tunnels to drink beer. Being San Francisco, marijuana is a popular choice as well, but John and his friends settled for drinking beer. The dark tunnels are out of the prying eyes of the police, a sanctuary. Things had certainly changed. He thinks back to when he was 14 and trying to get into SI. The pressure, the entry test, the required grades and community service… it was overwhelming. He wonders if Lucia was thinking about all those things when maybe she let her guard down, and this asshole grabbed her. He just didn't know.

He's been there long enough, so he starts up the car once again. This time, he crosses the bridge and goes home.

In front of his condo, Reggie climbs out the passenger side and reminds Kathy he will see her in the morning.

Once inside, Reggie re-heats some leftover Chinese food. He is on his second scotch and feeling quite melancholy. This case stirs up memories he had tried to forget. He remembers vividly his best friend's death so many years ago, the funeral, and mostly his friend's mom. He watched her being slowly eaten away by this thing, this death. Nothing could console her. He sees that same look on Mrs. Rosini's face, and, for that matter, Mr. Rosini's as well. He knows they will never recover. No matter what he does or how hard all the Inspectors work, the die was cast, the damage done. He feels helpless. All his skill and ability can't ease the pain. He throws the food in the garbage and pours a third scotch.

Before they leave Reggie's place, from the back seat, Liam suggests that Kathy might want to slide over and let him drive. She is too tired to argue, shifts to the passenger seat and closes her eyes. Liam drives to the 280 Freeway entrance and heads south. He gets off at

Westlake and heads for their favorite place, Westlake Joe's. Kathy has fallen asleep, and only begins waking up as Liam is parking the car. She looks up and sees where they were. "Great choice! This is perfect. Thank you."

They walked from the parking lot, through the front doors, and straight to the check-in podium. As usual, the restaurant is packed. It's amazing what great food and exceptional service can do for the bottom line. Liam explains to the maître'd that they don't have a reservation, but after a drink, they would be happy with seats at the counter. The maître'd says that won't be a problem. Liam takes Kathy's hand, and they turn to the left and enter the bar. The bartender, George, immediately greets them, not quite with the enthusiasm of Norm entering *Cheers*, but welcoming all the same!

A gentleman seated between two empty bar chairs saw them approaching and immediately moved over, so they could sit together... class. George, the consummate bartender, stood at the ready, asking, "A Cosmo up, and Jameson rocks?"

Liam stares at him, then turning to the gentleman who had switched his seat. "Amazing, and I've only been in here once before." George laughs. "Of course, you're right on both drinks, and please, another of whatever this fine gentleman is drinking." The gentleman raised his almost empty glass in a thank-you salute. Kathy looks at George and asks, "May I have a glass of the Bohemian Vineyard Pinot Noir instead?"

"No problem, Jameson rocks and Bohemian Pinot Noir."

Liam and Kathy sit down. George has their drinks ready in record time. "You guys look like you need a drink. Bad day?"

Kathy looks up. "You read about the little girl that is missing?"

George replies, "You mean the firefighter's kid?"

"The very same. We caught that case."

"Wow, that's tough."

"And...we found her body this morning...she was murdered."

"How 'bout I see if I can get you moved up for dinner?"

"That's OK, we told the maître d we were going to just sit at the counter," Liam said.

"Got it."

George leaves them and moves up and down the bar, making friends and satisfying customers. Liam spots him talking to the maître'd while at the cash register. Kathy turns. "I needed this. You're a mind reader."

Liam motions to George to bring Kathy another, and switches to club soda for himself.

He looks at Kathy and suggests, "I'll drive, you can relax, I'm now on club soda."

She took his hand. "I sound like a broken record, but thank you."

Kathy is well into her second glass of wine and Liam is nursing his club soda when the maître'd appears and alerts them of a cancellation. "You now have a quiet table in the secondary dining room if you want it," he said.

Liam and Kathy finish their drinks and get up to follow the maître'd. George tells them he would transfer their bar tab to the dinner bill. Kathy passes in front of Liam as he puts $20 on the bar and asks George if he could recall, before tonight, a cancellation?

George clears their glasses and wipes the bar. "Happens all the time."

Liam smiles. "Right, and thank you."

Liam and Kathy share a wonderful dinner – Chicken Marsala for Kathy, and Joe's House Made Ravioli for Liam. Kathy, now accompanied by her very own designated driver, and in honor of her Chicken Marsala, switched wines. Liam said he'd have a glass as well, so they ordered a bottle of Cleary Ranch Chardonnay.

Kathy tells Liam about the notification at the Rosini home, and how horrible it had been. Liam can only listen; it is obvious she just needs to talk. "Lucia was just like me and probably ten of my closest friends growing up," she says. "We were all so excited about high school and beginning to be on our own. It just doesn't seem possible someone could just kill her."

Liam tells her it might hurt more for just that reason, because Lucia really is like Kathy and her friends. He reminds her that it's also close to home because Dad is a firefighter and the Rosini's are like family. "They are fortunate it is you who told them. They see who you are and that you really do care. They know they're in good, caring hands," he said.

Tears pool in her eyes. "Thanks for listening. I think I feel a little better."

They finish their dinner and Kathy finished the last of the Chardonnay. Liam looks at her. "At this rate, I may get lucky tonight."

Kathy, looking very comfortable and a bit tipsy, stares over the rim of her wine glass,

"Only if you're into necrophilia."

As they are leaving, they pass the maître'd. Liam tips him and thanks him for everything. Liam holds on to Kathy as they walk to their car for the drive back to Noe Valley. Once the car is in motion, Kathy falls sound asleep. When they arrive at the condo, Liam wakes her and helps her to bed. He hangs up everyone's clothes, prepares the kitchen for tomorrow, and walks back to the bedroom. She actually looks strangely peaceful after her terrible day.

As he prepares to join her, he thinks she won't be so peaceful in the morning.

He climbs into bed... and there is no necrophilia.

CHAPTER 19

The Conference Room is full as the task force gathers. Danny sits at the head of the table.

"Okay," he says, "let's start a To Do list."

Kathy reaches for a legal pad on the table and pops the cap from a pen. She looks around her and shrugs, "I was really good at taking notes in college."

"I'll start," Danny says. "Let's run every person that's been interviewed so far through all our databases. Let's concentrate on lists of prior sex offenders and pedophiles."

As Kathy quickly writes, John speaks up. "We need a team to go back and get the names of every person working in any open business during what we feel is the time of the abduction."

"We need to interview all the Muni drivers on the 30 Stockton working that day," Reggie says. "I know it's a long shot, but it has to be done."

"Back to the school…" Kathy didn't recognize the voice, and didn't take the time to look up. "…and this time all the classmates. Did anyone see anything out of the ordinary?"

"Re-interview William, our homeless Material Witness. Maybe he remembers something more."

"It looks like there may have been some work done on the church during that critical time," Liam said. "It looks like the work's complete now. We should get a list of contractors, subcontractors, and all the people who worked on the project. Those people also need to be run through all the databases."

"Re-interview Ann and Claire," John added. "Now that it's a murder, maybe we can jar some additional memories loose."

As Kathy finished writing the last point, she thought of something. "We need the autopsy and forensic results in case we get lucky and they can supply a new direction."

"Good," Danny said. "That should keep us busy for a while. And one more thing," he leaned back in his chair. "I know this one is going to piss off everyone in the room, but I'm going to bring in the Bureau."

A few groans sound around the room. Danny nods and held his hands up. "I know they're a bunch of pompous asses, but unfortunately, it's the culture of that organization, and in spite of that culture, there are a lot of great agents. Plus, they have their Missing and Exploited Children's Task Force out of DC, and they have the best database in the country.

Besides that, you all know the good ones, you've worked with them before; seek them out."

More sighs rose from the group, but they all agreed that no turf issue should get in the way of solving the case.

"Alright, so let's get started." Danny stands up. "John and Liam, hand out the assignments and be sure each one is logged into the computer for this case. We all meet back here at 5:00 pm, unless you're in the middle of an interview."

Everyone nods their acknowledgment and agreement as Danny leaves the room. He unconsciously slumped heavily as he walked down the hallway. What has started out as a Missing Persons case has turned into quite the shit show. Whenever a pretty young girl is abducted, raped, and killed, public sympathy for the family and the degree of indignation is high, even on a national level. The pressure on the San Francisco Police Department to solve the case will be enormous.

Danny arrives at the Chief's office to find the door open. He rapped a couple of times on the doorjamb before entering.

"Please tell me we have something," Chief Walker says.

Danny takes a deep breath. "The body is at the Medical Examiner's. All evidence, what there is of it, is at the lab, and Toxicology is working on a rush order. We're all over the scene at Lincoln Park. We're checking all the people we talked to last night against every database we can find. We're going back to the school and the neighborhood, as we speak. The family's been notified, and I took the liberty of bringing the Bureau and their Missing Children's Task Force in on the case. We should have several additional agents to help within the next few hours. I'm meeting with SAC Newell when I leave here."

"Okay. Newell's a good man; he's a team player. What's next?"

"I think we should get ahead of the press on this. Regular updates will let us control the information flow and still give the media access and information. This is already national, so we may see some of the big guns. Maybe add another PIO so one is always available. Our task force has been told, under penalty of death, that this case will be discussed with no one, no exceptions."

CHAPTER 20

Even as Danny is looking over reports from other Bureaus — a string of robberies culminating in a homicide in Russian Hill, a fatal hit-and-run on the Embarcadero — he isn't entirely focused. His mind is absorbed with the Lucia Rosini murder, fully focused on it.

There's a knock at his door. He looks up to see FBI Special Agent in Charge, Robert Newell.

"Danny, good to see you again."

"Bob," Danny smiles, stands, and extends his hand. "Thanks for coming."

"You call, I come."

Danny gestures to one of the chairs in front of his desk. "Have a seat."

Newell sits down and gives Danny his full attention. "We wanted to bring you and your Missing Children's Task Force into this investigation if you're available," Danny says.

"That's what we're here for, despite rumors to the contrary."

That brings a wry smile to Danny's face. Newell continues, "The Task Force has some great people, and their data collection is second to none. I took the liberty of making the formal request with the Assistant Director, and she gave me the go ahead to talk to the Task Force SAC directly."

Danny folds his hands on the desk and leans forward. "I think it's wise to clear the air, and to address the aforementioned skepticism on Bureau assistance. It's not that folks don't think you're here to help, it's just that, well, sometimes that helping hand involves taking over the investigation. Be that as it may, I appreciate your being here and making the call to Quantico."

"You know me better than that, Danny. Your case, your call. We're part of a team.

Anyway, I brought twelve agents here with me to begin working with your people. Force will fly in this afternoon. Newell looks at his watch, actually in a few minutes. I'll get them situated and they'll be here in the morning. I believe they're sending four agents and two profilers. And yes, just like TV, they do actually have a plane."

Danny thinks a minute.

"How about I have them picked up as soon as they land and bring them here. They can get a head start, and then you can get them situated. Maybe a little bonding with a couple of my Inspectors on the ride here."

"That works for me, sounds like a plan." Danny makes the call.

"I know you have the latest version of the Case Management System that was developed to track every aspect of a case from reports to forensics," Danny said. "Any chance you could bring that with you? If we could download it to our laptops, we could all communicate in real time and everyone could access the case material."

"I thought you already had that software. I distinctly remember it being pirated from us on that Tenderloin Task Force, where that psycho was stabbing prostitutes. We were lucky we got out of here with our cars and radios."

Danny holds his hands up in mock protest. "I can neither confirm nor deny any acts of piracy, but the alleged pirated version is Case Management 1.0. I'm betting you guys are on version 10 by now."

Newell smiled. "That's probably true, and yes, we'll bring it, and we'll get everyone on the same page."

"Good. Thank you."

"So, who's running the case, boots on the ground?"

"Inspectors O'Neill, Donnelly, Sullivan, and Gibson."

"Wow, big fan of diversity, are you?" Newell flashed another smile. "Tell me one's from Northern Ireland."

"I know," Danny replied, "but they're good. We have a contingent from Missing Persons, Juvenile, and Narcotics assigned as well."

"I know they're good, I've worked with all four on other investigations. Why Narcotics? You keeping something from the press?"

Danny shook his head. "No, no drug connection. We just needed people who could go on the street and interview a number of the homeless community without spooking the entire camp."

Newell nods in agreement. "My people would definitely be out on that one. How 'bout Forensics and a cause of death?"

"Everything we've found, which is the girl's body dumped in a large plastic construction bag in the shrubs off the tenth green at Lincoln Park, is at the lab. Preliminary Cause of Death (COD) is strangulation. She was also hit in the face and, based on the blood, the blow to the face was first. They're running the Toxicology as a rush, but I don't think we're going to find anything. The girl was a good student, good daughter, good sister, good friend. All-American girl, and Dad's a firefighter here in the city."

Newell shook his head, visibly saddened. "Wow, that hurts. That's losing family. Well, you'll have my people in a few hours." He pulls a card out of his pocket and hands it to Danny. "Here's my cell. Call if there are any turf issues."

"Thanks, Bob." Danny picks one of his cards from the holder on his desk and turns it over, writing on the back. "Here's my number. You call me if any of your people are made to feel anything other than welcome and included. Would you like to see what we have so far?"

"Absolutely."

"Come with me."

Danny leads him down to the Conference Room. It is crowded, standing room only, with 20 SFPD personnel from various Bureaus, Assistant District Attorney Hernandez, clerical and IT people, and the twelve recently arrived FBI agents along with a couple of Command Officers.

"Okay, everyone," Danny says over the din of voices, "let's quiet down. I'd tell you to take a seat, but there clearly aren't enough. I'll try to get us a bigger room with more data connections. For now, though, let me introduce the inspectors who will be running the investigation on the street, and the Assistant Special Agent in Charge (ASAC) from the Bureau, who will be handling the FBI contingent. The ASAC and the Inspectors are the 'go to' people on this case. Danny makes the introductions.

"So, why don't we go around the table and lay out what's going on now. John?"

"Okay, we have some of our Missing Persons people running everyone we interviewed through all known databases. We're going back to Washington Square and we're going to get the names of every employee at every business in the immediate area. Then we're going to run those through the databases. Narcotics is going to re-interview the homeless, one of them may remember something now that they are sober."

"Good. Liam?"

"We need the businesses to give us the names of every company that delivers to their business. Then, you got it, we contact the delivery companies, get the names of the drivers and run them through the system."

"Juvenile is going back to the school and conducting more detailed interviews," Kathy says. "Our Chaplain and his people are working with the family. They're going to have to make funeral plans very shortly. We have a homeless guy who found the girl's phone. We don't think he had anything to do with it, but to be safe, he's on ice as a Material Witness."

A brief disturbance follows as the door is opened, bumping the people standing near it. Reggie comes in, leading six FBI agents. "Boys and girls," Reggie said as they squeezed into the room, "these distinguished individuals have just flown out here from Quantico, may I present the Bureau's Missing and Exploited Children's Task Force. These three are Agents Andrews, Shaeffer, and Wilson; this is Supervisory Agent Clark, and the two agents on the left are Agent Profilers Baker and O'Connor."

A voice followed from the back of the room, in fullest County Cork brogue. "We'll not be so sure about the rest of you people, but O'Connor, you're welcome here any time." With that, profiler Mary Ellen O'Connor took a bow.

"The Chief is pulling out all the stops on this," Danny said after the laughter died down. "The victim is one of our firefighters' kids. We have to get this bastard, we have to do it quickly, and the case has to be airtight. ADA Hernandez has been assigned to this task force, and you need to run questions about any legal issues through him. No one is going to walk on a technicality."

"I want to thank SAC Newell for his support and for the agents and profilers assigned to this case. Between SFPD and the Bureau, we have the personnel, the equipment, the budget, and the expertise to solve this case." He chuckled. "When is the last time you heard that? I'll work on getting a bigger room and now I'll turn this over to the working folks."

"Any chance we could have this room for our people," ASAC Clark asked," once you get a bigger one for the whole group?"

"Most of us have been known to shower," Liam said.

"We're not being antisocial," Clark said, smiling at Liam's joke. "It's just that we can use a quiet space on occasion. You know space for the Ouija Board and Crystal Ball."

Again, from the back of the room, "Hey, the Bureau guy made a funny… at least I think he did."

Danny already had his cell in his hand to call the Chief. He's covered his other ear as the noise in the room increases as assignments are being handed out to the various personnel. As people file out of the room, Danny put his phone away.

"Chief says we can have the big classroom in Training," he says. "It's huge, with plenty of chairs, restrooms, computer data ports, white boards, overhead projectors, the whole nine yards." He turned to Clark. "And yes, your profilers can have this room."

"Sounds great," Clark smiles. "Thank you, sir."

CHAPTER 21

"Lieutenant?"

Danny looks up from the mass of papers littering his desk to see Jenny Robbins from Forensics standing in front of him. "Yes, Jenny. Come in."

"Sir, we have our findings on your homicide victim."

"Excellent! Let's have it."

"I'm afraid we don't have a smoking gun, but I'll give you what we do have." She pauses for a moment, gathering her thoughts. "We reviewed the contents of a large, construction-grade plastic bag. The victim had been placed in the bag along with her school uniform skirt, blouse, her shoes, socks, and her underwear. There is also a women's dark blue coat in the bag. The skirt has apparently been cut with a knife with a 4- to 5-inch blade. The underwear is also cut off.

"There are traces of blood on the blouse, enough that we were able to test it. It matched the victim's DNA. We understand she had been struck, and this amount of blood would be consistent with that report."

She pauses as she looked at the paper. "Go on," Danny says.

"Well, there's not a great deal more, but there are a couple of things that don't ring true. First, there's the presence of what appears to be construction dust on the victim's skirt, coat, and shoes - a combination of drywall dust, sawdust, things like that. We don't know where she could have come in contact with that type of material, and there isn't any in the bag."

"Also, in the corner of the bag is a rolled-up receipt from Cole's Hardware for $23.45. It doesn't say what was purchased, but it's dated the day before the girl went missing."

"Lastly, we found small traces of blood on the outside of the plastic bag, and that blood is not the victim's. It's enough for DNA analysis, but we don't know whose blood it is, as we didn't get any hits in our databases."

"Okay," Danny says, recounting the clues to impress them in his mind. "Our suspect has a knife, the victim has her clothes cut off, there's construction dust on her skirt, jacket, and shoes. She bled onto her blouse, and the blood is confirmed to be hers. We have a receipt from a hardware store. And we have an unknown person's blood on the outside of the plastic bag."

"That's correct, sir."

"Thank you, Jenny. I know this is a huge rush job and we appreciate everything."

Jenny hands him the report and leaves him to digest the findings. As he gets to the bottom of the sheet, he rubs his hand over his chin. Jenny is right, there isn't a great deal. Just a number of clues, but none really pointing him toward anything specific.

He stands up and grabs his jacket from the back of his chair. Maybe the Medical Examiner will have some answers.

Before he goes to the ME's office, Danny stops by Liam's desk and gave him the evidence bag with the Cole's Hardware receipt. "See if anyone at the Hardware store can shed some light on this purchase. It may be nothing, but let's be sure."

Dr. Goldberg, the Medical Examiner, had just settled down at his desk with an open file folder in front of him when Danny enters.

"Doc, tell me you've got the results on our victim."

"I just finished." Goldberg looks up at Danny, peering at the Lieutenant over the top of his reading glasses. "Have a seat. Sad case."

"I know. So, tell me something that will let us nail this asshole."

Goldberg sits back in his chair, looking down at the file. "Our victim is a perfectly healthy, normal, 14-year-old female. She was struck, probably with a closed fist, in the mouth area and the nose, two blows. She was forcibly raped. However, no semen was recovered. There are traces of spermicide present, so I'd say a condom."

"There are ligature marks on her wrists and ankles, consistent with some type of flex tie. There is evidence of petechial hemorrhaging, consistent with strangulation. And the bruising on her throat is consistent with finger marks, indicating manual strangulation. Her mouth was raw, consistent with the application of a gag. Stomach contents revealed a recently consumed cannoli.

"And the suspect was wearing latex gloves, with a powdered interior."

"I get everything but the latex gloves with powder," Danny said. "How did you come up with that?"

"Our victim was punched with a closed fist in the mouth area. The blow loosened a tooth, but before being displaced, that tooth cut the latex glove, leaving a small piece of latex with powder on one side."

"In my professional opinion, judging by the angle of the blow, your killer is right-handed, and I'll bet his right knuckle is cut. There are also black fibers in her hair, so I'm guessing a hood."

"Well, this is great, Doc," Danny says, trying to hide his disappointment. He wishes sometimes that real-life police investigations turned out like TV shows, where a unique fiber or exotic material of some kind pointed them without doubt, to the guilty party. "Did we get anything from Toxicology?"

Goldberg turns to a sheet in the file. "All the results aren't in, but there are no traces, not even a tiny amount of drugs in our victim's body. There are, however, traces of chloroform around her mouth. She was grabbed, drugged, tied up and gagged. Then she was beaten and raped, and finally strangled. She is a healthy, drug- alcohol- and smoke-free young woman, normal in every way."

"Thanks, Doc." Danny stands up. "As usual, you've been a big help."

"I didn't like doing this one." Goldberg takes his glasses off and looks up at Danny, concern and sadness in his eyes, his forehead wrinkling into a washboard. "Please catch this sick son of a bitch and allow me to ply my trade on his remains."

Danny smiles grimly, "Deal."

CHAPTER 22

Multiple cars converge on Washington Square as the SFPD and FBI personnel arrive to conduct their follow-up interviews.

"What the hell?" John exclaimed. Two fire engines and the Battalion Chief's car are double-parked in front of the church.

"Firefighters are all over the park," Liam points out.

"Yeah, this doesn't look like a fire or medical issue." John unfastens his seat belt and opens his door. "I'm going to find the Battalion Chief."

"Okay, partner. I'll get everyone started here."

The Battalion Chief is overseeing firefighters from the edge of the park a little farther down Filbert Street. John approaches him and presented his badge. "Chief, what are the firefighters doing in the park? Is there a fire or a medical issue?"

"No, we're just shaking up these assholes a bit. I know at least one of them knows what happened to Lucia, and we're damn sure going to find out."

"No, you're not," John insists. "Pack up your people and get the hell out of here."

"We're not budging," the Battalion Chief replies. He turns to squarely face John. "We have every right to be here, and we're going to get answers, even if you guys can't."

"Chief, you're compromising our efforts. What if we had an arson where a police officer's child died in the fire; how would you feel if I brought down a bunch of officers and walked through your arson scene?"

"This is different."

"It's no different. Now, I'm going to be as polite as possible. Please remove your people from the park. They're hurting our investigation."

"No, son, we're staying."

John turned and pulled out his phone. "Lieutenant," he said when Danny picked up, "we have a couple of engine companies and a Battalion Chief out here interfering with our investigation."

"What? Interfering with our investigation?"

"I mean, not directly, but they're out here conducting an investigation of their own. The firefighters may be well-meaning, but they're scaring off the homeless people we need to talk to, and God knows where they'll go from here, or if we'll even find them again."

"Have you ordered them out?"

"So far I've only asked, and asked very nicely, I might add. But this guy is a fucking Neanderthal. Probably is a B Company, Truckee, early in his career."

"A what?"

"Sorry," John said, "a fire department inside joke. B Company gets blamed for everything, and it's always the Truckees who are deep in the mix. I've got cousins on the job in the fire department."

"Okay, stay put for a minute. I need to make a call. By the way, where's Liam?"

"He's coordinating the re-canvass while I talk to this asshole."

"Keep him out of this. We don't need the arrest of two engine companies and a BC, and Liam will do just that."

"Agreed, but if this clown doesn't get the hell out of here, you're going to have your mass arrest and it won't be Liam."

"I understand. Give me a minute."

Chief Walker didn't like getting involved in conflicts with the Fire Department. It's like clashing with family. But they couldn't have any interference with their investigation, well-meaning though it may be.

Fire Chief Cavaglieri picked up, and Walker greeted him. "Chief, this is Mike Walker, SFPD."

Chiefs Walker and Cavaglieri are veterans of many wars with the Mayor and the Board of Supervisors. They learned early on there is safety in numbers, and that two heads are better than one. This is particularly true during budget or election season, when the politicians' need for 'ink' on page one, above the fold, frequently outweighed common-sense decisions. Unlike some cities, where the police and fire departments fought pitched battles on budgetary issues, Chiefs Walker and Cavaglieri had learned the value of working in tandem.

The Chiefs know the winds of financial good fortune are fickle, and the largesse of the Federal government toward cities and city departments changes yearly depending on the headlines. Starting a few years ago, with crime on the rise, the police are the favorite child, and received the bulk of the federal money. Now, it is the fire service. With the California wildfires and natural disasters nationwide, fire is first in line for the federal dollars. The two Chiefs have decided they would share the federal good fortune each year on programs that would run through one department but benefit both. It was the very definition of collaboration, and both agencies were the beneficiaries.

The Chiefs began their work by meeting privately at one of their homes and went over the budgets for both departments. Each would lay out their respective priorities and must-haves, and each brought along pre-determined throwaways, items they might like, but could certainly live without. During the budget sessions, they left each other's priorities alone, pushed the combined programs, and feigned battle over the throwaways. This kept the perceived turf wars in play for the Supervisors, allowing the Board to concentrate on mediating the 'red herrings', looking Solomon-like to their constituencies, while passing the priority portions unscathed. It is amazing someone hadn't thought of it before.

"Good morning, Chief. I assume you're calling about the Rosini investigation."

"I am. I need to talk to you about a group of fire department vigilantes, headed up by one of your overzealous battalion chiefs."

"Are you kidding me?"

"No, I'm afraid not. You have at least two engine companies and a BC in Washington Square Park actively interfering with this homicide investigation."

"Shit. I'm not aware of any such action."

"I'm sure you're not," Chief Walker says diplomatically. "Just check your status board and see where your people are located."

There is a brief pause, then Chief Cavaglieri is back. "I don't believe it."

"Yeah, I didn't either. Please get on the phone – no radio. So far, the press isn't there, and we'd like to keep it that way. We don't need Channels 2, 4, 5, 7, 11; or anyone else who may be listening, showing up for this little dustup."

"I'll do that right now."

Chief Walker nods. "I appreciate your help. And just an FYI; tell your BC that he was one step away from a jail cell. Had it been one of my less patient inspectors, that BC's call to you would have been one of the two he would have been allowed at booking."

"I'll definitely let him know. I'll get them out of there so you can get your work done. Thanks for the heads up."

"Thank you."

A minute later, Danny gets John back on the line. "Chief Walker has a couple of requests for you. He wants to know when the firefighters leave the park. And he wants that BC's name and where he's assigned. He'll be dealt with later, out of the prying eyes of witnesses."

"The BC just picked up his phone," John says. "He doesn't look very happy."

"I'm guessing he's going to be assigned to the Geary Street Firehouse, counting seagulls for the remainder of his once stellar career."

"He's calling everyone back to the rigs. Looks like they're getting ready to pull out. I just hope there isn't irreparable damage."

"Well, the Chief said to tell you that you did a great job of avoiding a black eye for both departments. No one would have come out of this looking like anything but a bunch of incompetent fools."

"Thank you, sir."

"I'll let you get back to your investigation. Oh, by the way," Danny added, "the Forensics crew found construction dust on the girl's skirt, shoes, and coat. Not sure what to make of that."

"Interesting," John pondered. "During the initial interviews the other night, witnesses said there were construction vans – plumbing, drywall, electric, paint – parked around the church over the past few weeks."

"Better check with the good Fathers and see what is going on. We might have a witness."

"We're on it. Thanks."

"This is so sad," Father Bernard says, his head bowed. John and Liam find him in front of the church, watching the Fire Department activity. "Lucia is a wonderful girl, wonderful family."

John nervously clears his throat in preparation for interrupting the priest's grief. "We are told there was construction going on here at the church at the time Lucia disappeared." He looks around. "But I don't see any of that now."

"That's right, we had a water leak at the rear of the Sacristy. It damaged the walls and even shorted out some of the electric. We had to call in contractors, last minute, to get things done quickly. They were very nice, even fixed a leaky faucet at the rear of the Rectory. They were all gone yesterday."

"Do you have the names of the contractors who worked on the church and Rectory?" Liam asked.

"I believe I have all that information in my office, if you will follow me back to the rectory."

The priest turns, and John and Liam begin following him up the steps. "Hey, look at this," Liam said to John, pointing at the steps. An accumulation of whitish dust has gathered in the seams and corners. "I'd guess that would qualify as construction dust."

"I'll buy that," John replies, as they run up the steps to catch up with the priest. "Isn't the story she sat on the steps to eat her pastry?"

"It is." Liam tries to keep his optimism in check. "This could be a dead end, but who knows, maybe someone saw something."

They followed the priest into his office where he opened a folder on his desk. "Here we are," he said. "There are four contractors. Leak Busters Plumbing, over on Chestnut. San Francisco Electric on Columbus near the old Tower Records. Bay Area Dry Wall, out in the

Mission. And.... hmmm, strange." He reaches for his phone and presses a button. "Monsignor Lombardi, would you mind coming to my office? Thank you."

"Father," Liam says, "you said there are four contractors, but I couldn't help but notice that you only named three."

"Yes, the fourth one is odd. Harris Painting."

"What's odd about it?"

"Usual procedure is we will issue a check for the work, based on an invoice. But on these invoices, the checks will not have gone out yet, as the job just finished. Yet this Harris Painting shows a 'paid in full' invoice, handwritten, and there's no address."

"Sloppy bookkeeping?" John posited.

"I'm not sure. I didn't sign off on this one. It is Monsignor Lombardi."

"Good day, gentlemen," said a voice from the door. "How can I assist you?"

"Monsignor," Father Bernard said, "these are Inspectors O'Neill and Donnelly from the Police Department. Gentlemen, Monsignor Lombardi."

Monsignor Lombardi walks into the room. He is a short man, probably no more than five-foot-seven; however, he is obviously no stranger to the culinary delights of the North Beach restaurants and Victoria's pastries. He will tip the scales in the heavyweight division, a good 240 pounds. He is wearing his Monsignor cassock with the purple trim.

"Hello, Monsignor," Liam says. "We are going over the construction invoices to try and identify anyone who worked on the emergency repair project. We're looking for potential witnesses in our murder investigation."

"Yes, of course. How can I help?"

"We show a 'paid in full' invoice to a Harris Painting for work done here at the church, but there's no address, and it's been paid before all the rest. According to Father Bernard, it appears to be your signature signing off the invoice. Can you explain why this one was handled in a different fashion?"

"Well, the first contractors were hard at work repairing the plumbing and electric, and the drywallers were patching things as fast as the plumbers and electricians tore them out. This is an old church, and it seems that every repair generated a new repair. It was becoming quite costly."

"Go on," John said.

"A painter approached me at the back and told me he'd seen the contractors' vans parked around the church, but he didn't see a painter. He said once those plumbers, electricians, and drywallers left, we would need a painter to put things back in their proper state. I guess I had been a little flustered. I hadn't really thought about it, so I told him to give me an estimate."

"Did he have a vehicle?" Liam asked.

"Yes, it was an older van with the name on the side. The lettering was kind of faded, though."

"Monsignor," John said, "please continue with the painter part of the story."

"Yes, well, he walked around the back of the church where all the work was being done and said he could do the job for $1,500. Well, I'm no contractor, but even I knew this is a bargain, given the amount of painting to be done. He said the only catch is that he needed cash and he needed to be paid immediately after the job was completed. That didn't seem unreasonable, and since the price was a huge help in offsetting the overages in the project, well, I agreed."

"Monsignor, do you have his name, a phone number, or maybe the license number on the van?"

Liam stands with his pen poised over his notebook.

Monsignor Lombardi approaches the desk and starts looking through the folder.

"The name should be here somewhere, but unless there's a phone number on the invoice, I'm afraid I don't know it. I didn't get a license plate either or, for that matter, his state contractor's license."

"Okay, what about the painter's name?"

"Here it is, Chester Wells."

"Could you describe this fellow, Monsignor?"

"Let's see," Monsignor Lombardi exhaled as he looked upwards, remembering. "He was white, about 45 to 50 years old. He had dark hair and it was cut short – not shaved, but something like a military cut. I'm five-foot-ten and he was just a bit taller, say six feet, and I'd guess about 180 pounds."

"Anything distinctive or out of the ordinary about him? Maybe a limp or an accent?"

"An accent. Trace of the Old South, maybe Alabama or Georgia."

"Great. Thanks for your help."

"I know I should have never let a potentially unlicensed contractor on the property," the Monsignor said with a worried tone, "but the price was so good, and look at the job he did. He's an exceptionally good painter."

"It's okay, Monsignor," John says, "we understand."

As they turn to leave, Liam remarks under his breath, "I guess the lawsuits are cutting into the church bank accounts."

Father Bernard walks quickly behind them. "Oh, Inspectors," he says, "there's a camera on the corner of the church. We put it there because of some late-night vandalism. If this painter came up Stockton Street, it may have captured the license plate."

"Thank you, Father," Liam says. "Any chance that footage is stored somewhere we could see it?"

"Yes, right this way."

Back in the priest's office, he goes to his computer and opens the application containing the security recordings. He spends a couple minutes locating the file, based on the dates the construction was going on. While scrolling through them, they see the Harris Painting van.

Excitement surges through John and Liam, but both have to quell that feeling as they continue watching. The rear license plate is not visible, nor is the driver. Every day, the van drives down Stockton on its arrival, without a front plate. The sun visor is pulled down each time, obscuring the driver's face. They skipped through more of same, speeding through the recording until they reached the last day and watched the van drive away for the last time.

"Thanks, Father," John sighed. "I thought we might have had something there."

"Wait a minute," Liam says. "If the camera picks up the van, any chance it might have seen our victim?"

"I'll back it up." Father Bernard scrolled back a couple days and begins playing the recording in fast speed. He slows it down when Lucia comes into view. She is walking up Stockton, next to the church. She stops and appears to be looking down the driveway, possibly talking to someone. After that conversation, she walks down the driveway and disappeared from the camera's view.

A short time later, the Harris Painting van leaves. Again, the plate isn't visible.

"Can you make a copy of that footage for us?" Liam asks.

"Certainly," Father Bernard says, pulling a small flash drive out of a drawer. "I can do that right now. I'm just sorry the camera didn't help with the van."

"Not your fault, Padre. Thanks for all your help. By the way, how long do you keep the footage before recording over it?"

"Thirty days, replies Father Bernard."

A few minutes later, Liam and John leave, stopping briefly to collect some of the dust on the front steps of the church into a small evidence bag.

CHAPTER 23

The Training Division's large classroom is reconfigured to accommodate the task force, their equipment and computers. Their next briefing is held in the room. Everyone seems more relaxed, as if they could get used to the accommodations, though the Lieutenant warns them against getting too comfortable, since it isn't going to be a permanent thing.

Danny calls the meeting to order. "We've gone over all the material that was collected today, and I want to take a minute to bring everyone up to speed on the Medical Examiner's report and the Forensics analysis. First, the cause of death is manual strangulation. She was drugged with chloroform, bound with zip ties, and gagged, and based on fiber evidence, probably had a hood over her head. Her clothes were cut off, and she was punched in the face at least twice, and raped. Her body, along with her clothes, was stuffed in a large plastic construction bag and dumped in the bushes between the tenth green and eleventh tee at Lincoln Park Golf Course."

"Question," says one of the agents borrowed from Narcotics. "If he is going to kill her, why a hood? Doesn't make sense."

Danny shakes his head. "I don't know. Maybe our profilers will have some answers. They'll be here in a minute."

"Forensics says that her skirt, shoes, and coat have construction dust on them. Also, there are trace amounts of blood on the outside of the bag that contained the body, and that blood is not our victim's. Interviews at the church indicate there was a construction project underway at the church, and it just recently concluded. There's construction dust on the stairs of the church, where we believe she sat, that we hope will be consistent with the dust on the victim's clothing.

We've recovered the victim's phone, and the GPS trace places the victim at the driveway at the rear of the church. Then it's on the move to the tunnels at the Presidio and the parking lot by the old gun batteries. From there it, we assume, drives around for a few minutes and stops again in the parking lot at the Legion of Honor and the golf course. From there, back to the trashcan on Columbus next to the park, where our homeless guy finds it. Forensics is still out at the Presidio looking for any evidence.

We have camera footage of our victim walking to the driveway at the rear of the church, then disappearing down the driveway. A painting van, Harris Painting, leaves a few minutes later."

A Missing Persons agent raised his hand. "Anything on the blood on the bag?"

"No hits, but it's a viable sample for DNA."

"Anything on Harris Painting?"

"No, nothing current. We checked business licenses, the Secretary of State registrations, Franchise Tax, and our own records. All we could find is a Harris Painting out of Oakland that went under some ten years ago. The owner of that company died a few years later. The company assets, including the vans, were auctioned off. One van is still registered, but it's registered in Gilroy, and Gilroy PD confirms that it's still there and the new owner is clean. However, we were able to get a description of the driver of the van: White male, 45 to 50, 6 feet tall, 180 pounds, short dark hair."

Liam speaks up. "We checked on the receipt found in the bag, and the clerk at Cole's Hardware says it is a single item, paint thinner. Cash purchase. He went on to say that he vaguely remembered the sale, and the guy was just an average guy; white, 45 or so, very average, wearing painter's coveralls. He can't ID him."

The door opens and the profilers enter the classroom and make their way toward empty desks. "Sorry we're late," said Baker.

"That's okay," Danny says. "As long as you're here, maybe you can give us an update on what you've found."

They glance at each other, and O'Connor spoke up. "I'll start by saying that this is not an exact science. Unlike the

TV show, we don't pull rabbits out of hats and then run out and kick down doors and shoot the suspects."

"That part's our job," Liam quipped.

"That said, we believe, based on everything you have un-covered so far, that our responsible party is most likely a white male, probably between the ages of 40 and 50. He'll be a loner with few or no friends. He probably travels freely and has no ties to any one place. He's careful, which indicates that he's done this before. He's not stupid and he knows about forensics, hence the precautions on prints and fibers.

We feel that he's done this often enough that we'll likely categorize him as a serial killer. We saw the part about the suspected hood, and we think he started out using a hood to keep from being identified and not killing his victims. Now that he's evolved into a killer, it's just force of habit.

"We're running his MO against every database we can find, both here in the U.S. and Canada, Mexico, and even Interpol. So far, nothing that matches the DNA from the plastic bag in your case."

"That's spooky," John whispers to Liam.

"No shit."

Baker picks up the narrative. "Our team is trying to iden-tify similar cases nationwide that don't have DNA evidence, and looking at rape abductions where the victims survive. For expediency's sake, we're looking at the rape/abductions/with survivors that precede this rape/abduction/homicide. As you can imagine, there are a lot of cases and we also must rely on the reporting agency to correctly categorize the crime so it gets looked at. Sometimes in small, very rural departments, this is an issue, and unfortunately some of our suspects start out in small, rural areas."

"I want to thank all of you for everything you have done so far," Danny said. "We have a potential suspect, we have DNA, and we have evidence. We just need to connect all the dots."

"Tomorrow's the funeral. We'll have a detail there, complete with cameras, video, audio, and any other technology I can scam. The Bureau's bringing their best AV stuff as well. Go home, get a good night's sleep, and we meet back here tomorrow morning at 7:30 a.m. to get our assignments for the day."

A few groans follow as several of the agents and officers stand up, attesting to the fact that it had been another long day.

"You want me to drop you off?" John asked Reggie.

"That sounds great," Reggie sighed. "I'm dead."

"Yeah, I hear you. And I have a feeling tomorrow is going to be a busy day."

"What scares me," Liam says, "is having the DNA of a possible suspect, and no one to match it to. I don't want to be part of a case that goes cold, and then some asshole gets picked up for back alimony, 25 years from now, and it's a DNA match. Then *60 Minutes* will send a crew out to the Old Folks Home, interviewing the original investigators."

"I think I'd still be a good interview," Kathy mused. "Dynamic female Assistant Chief. You'd be face down in a bowl of Pablum."

"Very funny," Liam scoffs. "But seriously, though, I don't want this to be an unsolved cold case. I don't want this one following me around, despite the efforts of the dynamic inspector, who couldn't even spell Deputy Chief."

"Let's get out of here," Kathy says. "I'm hungry and tired and..." Her unfinished thought hangs in the air, but she couldn't complete the thought.

"Yeah, me too."

CHAPTER 24

"I'll stop by my place first, get some clean clothes and water the plants. Then we can head back to your place, grab some takeout, and get comfortable."

Liam smiles. "Sounds good to me. I'll call ahead and order while you're getting your clothes and taking care of the horticulture. How 'bout Chinese?"

"Mmm," Kathy said as she pulled up in front of her house. "Sounds perfect. Broccoli beef, lemon chicken, and rice."

"And some chicken egg foo young. I'm on it."

Liam then got busy on his phone and barely noticed Kathy getting out of the car. A couple of minutes later, she is back, and placing her clothes in the back seat. After a quick stop for the Chinese takeout, they arrive at Liam's condo a few minutes later.

"I'm going to take a shower," Kathy says, carrying her clothes into the bedroom.

"Okay, babe. I'll set the table and I'll be right behind you."

Liam grabbed a couple plates from the cabinet, places them on the table with the takeout cartons, and opens a bottle of the Cleary Ranch Chardonnay. He starts taking his shirt off as he walks into the bedroom, and stops as he passed the open bathroom door. He can see Kathy through the glass door of the shower, and takes in her figure for a minute. There is something very erotic about watching her rub her hands over her naked body, washing herself. He decides he better stop watching and get undressed if he wants to have a hand in that.

He opened the shower door and stepped in; his body partly shielded from the hot spray by Kathy. She turns toward him, and Liam takes a long moment to appreciate her anatomy, slippery and unencumbered by clothing. Soon lip-locked, they engaged in some moves that involved soap and, to a certain extent, resembled washing.

By the time they are finished, they are aroused and anxious to get under the covers. They take a couple of minutes to quickly dry off, and then stumbled together to the bedroom, where they collapse on the bed. Despite his fatigue, Liam's hands become occupied with their tactile exploration of the soft curves of Kathy's body, and he grows happier when her hands began a similar exploration of their own. After a couple of minutes, they pull close, each holding the other in a tight, loving embrace. They hold the embrace just a little too long, though. Before they can pull away and allow the natural progression of their lovemaking to take over, they are both fast asleep.

Liam looks at the illuminated numbers on his bedside clock. Nearly 3:00 a.m. He carefully, quietly, rolls out of bed and pads into the kitchen. All the lights are still on, the food cartons are on the table, and the wine is warm. *God, we were more shot than I realized*, Liam thought.

He gathers up the food and wine and places them in the refrigerator. As long as he is in the kitchen, he figures he'll get a jump on breakfast, so he takes cups and silverware from the cabinet and drawers. He put a K-cup and water in the Keurig, and prepped it for the first cup.

Still naked, he is getting a little chilled, so he returns to the bedroom. It felt good to slip back in bed, snuggling up to Kathy, careful not to wake her, hoping to catch a few more hours of rest.

But he can't get back to sleep. Thoughts of the investigation march through his head, the steps he still needs to take. He feared there may be something he missed. Then he thinks about that poor family. Were Mr. and Mrs. Rosini asleep now, snuggled up in each other's arms? Or were they lying awake, preparing themselves for the funeral?

It takes nearly an hour to fall back to sleep.

It is dark at the Rosini home. Tomorrow is the funeral. Mrs. Rosini pretended to be asleep, but she wonders if she will ever sleep again. She hears her husband get up and walk to the kitchen, but she still feigns sleep. Her thoughts are a montage of images of her beautiful daughter, her first day at school, her First Communion, her Confirmation, her cat, her helping in the kitchen, the day she applied to St. Ignatius, all happy and so full of promise.

Then there are the images she just can't shake, her little girl, scared, terrified, alone, and calling for her mother. Finally, a dark shadow, blocking out the images of Lucia, silencing her cries for help... how could this happen?

She shakes her head. *It is my fault.*

Downstairs, Mr. Rosini sits in the kitchen, like he did any night Lucia is out. He always waits up for her and she always comes home on time. Lucia, never a problem, always the good girl... Daddy's girl. So why didn't he protect her? How could he let a stranger take his little girl? How can he let someone defile her, hurt her, frighten her? He knows she called out for him... where is he? *How can I have let her down?* It is nearing daylight as he climbed back into bed, taking care to be quiet. His wife turns to him, reaches out and buries her head on his chest and cries. He holds her, and cries with her.

After getting up and preparing breakfast, Liam places a buttered English muffin on Kathy's plate, already laden with eggs and sausage.

"What happened last night?" Kathy asks. "I remember being exceptionally clean after my shower, very comfortable next to you in bed... and then waking up this morning."

"Yeah, we went out like the proverbial lights. I woke up around 3:00 and cleaned up the kitchen, and then I came back to bed. Had trouble sleeping, though. This case is really getting to me."

"I know, Kathy mused, "And today will be doubly tough. I keep thinking there's something out there we just haven't found yet."

"I'm worse. I'm thinking there may be something that I missed."

Kathy ponders over Liam's concern, trying to identify any missing pieces. "I don't know. We have Forensics, the Medical Examiner's report, the neighborhood canvass, the witness interviews, the retrace of the victim's last hours, the surveillance footage from the church, and today we'll surveille the funeral. We've got DNA, and the Bureau is pulling similar cases nationwide. What can we be missing?"

"I don't know." Liam takes a sip of coffee. "I'm going to go to the AV folks and have them show me all the footage they retrieved from the neighborhood surveillance cameras. Maybe we missed something. I want to go back over the ME's report and, and . . . Shit, I don't know.

There must be something. This asshole can't get away."

Kathy nods sympathetically as she finished her breakfast. "Well," she said, wiping her mouth on her napkin, "I'm off to pick up Reggie. I'll see you at work, sweetheart."

"Okay."

Liam pushes his chair back from the table. Kathy looks at him and feels drawn to him, enough to go and kiss him goodbye. As she bends over, Liam pulls her down into his lap and gives her more than just the peck she was hoping for. When they pull apart, Kathy looks at him, slightly breathless. "What are you still doing here?" he asked.

Kathy smiles and pushes herself up. She gathers up her things and leaves.

A few minutes later, John pulls up and, as usual, Liam has travel mugs of coffee for each of them.

"Thanks." John takes his mug and sips. "I really need coffee this morning. When I got home last night, I sat down and just picked at my dinner. Susan asked how the case is going and I filled her in." He paused for a moment. "I keep thinking we missed something. It kept me up half the night."

"Me too," Liam acknowledged. "I was up at 3:00. I'm going to go over the surveillance footage with the AV people, then I'm going to reread the ME's report."

"I'll go and make nice with the profilers," John said, "and see where they are. As much as I hate to admit it, they're pretty helpful. Not like that goofy TV show."

"I agree," Liam said. "And I want their plane."

The rest of the drive is mostly quiet and thoughtful. As John pulls into the parking garage, he sums up their plans. "Okay, so we split up, and then we'll meet in the office before the morning briefing."

Liam nods. "See you then."

CHAPTER 25

Liam feels like a tennis spectator, his head swiveling back and forth, as he watches the two monitors in the SFPD Audio Visual Department. The AV tech continues playing surveillance footage from businesses, residences, cell phones and traffic cameras; anything they were able to round up in connection with the case.

"Where's this footage from?" Liam asked, pointing to one of the monitors.

The AV tech looked up. "A little grocery store about a block up Stockton Street from the church. I've gone there myself. Good deli."

"Okay… on the day in question, we can see a van leave the driveway of the church at the right time, but the sun visor's down, and you can't see the driver."

"Right."

"Any chance we have video from the days leading up to the abduction? Maybe this asshole isn't as careful on some other day and left the visor up when he left."

"Give me a couple of minutes to upload the video."

The tech begins checking the video files. He finds the one he wants and opens it, dragging the button on the progress bar to about a week prior to the abduction. He showed Liam how to operate the machine so he could look at the footage he wanted, at his own viewing speed. As the tech went about other business, Liam scrolls through the video, watching for the Harris Painting van.

Time passes uneventfully, which starts to frustrate Liam. "Come on," he mutters. "The Church footage shows you arriving with the visor down, and this one shows you leaving with the visor still down, even though the sun is behind you." He shook his head. "You're one clever bastard. But you're going to fuck up, and I'll catch you."

He glances at his watch and signals the tech that he is finished for now. The morning's briefing would be starting in a few minutes.

Liam heads back toward Homicide, glancing at the ME's report. He sees the part about the torn piece of latex glove lodged against Lucia's damaged tooth, and he stops, holding up the photo. He reads the description of the latex, with the smear of blood on it. Something is teasing his brain, a question beginning to form. Rather than heading to the Training Room, he goes to his desk. He picked up the phone and called Forensics.

"Liam Donnelly, Homicide. In the Lucia Rosini case, has this piece of latex recovered from the victim's mouth been sent out for DNA testing?"

"No," the Forensics Analyst replies, "we still have it here."

"Can you send it out for me? Put a rush on it."

"You got it."

"Thanks."

He hangs up just as John arrives in the office. "Ready?"

"Absolutely!"

They walk to the Training Room and find a couple of seats. Nearly everyone else is already there, and the room is almost full. Danny comes in just behind them.

"Okay," the lieutenant says, getting right to business, "no new developments overnight, after yesterday's interviews and re-interviews with all the businesses by the park. It's lucky we're a Sanctuary City or after all the police activity over the past evenings, there probably wouldn't be a dishwasher or busboy back to work in any restaurant in a five-mile radius."

He turns to the Profilers. "Any luck on the databases?"

"This guy's DNA isn't in any database we have access to," Baker replies, "and that just doesn't make sense. We know he's done this before, and we can't believe that he hasn't been caught somewhere. We have people hand-searching every case on file that sounds remotely like this one, looking for the break we need."

"Good. Keep us apprised."

Other details of the investigation are shared, but so far, no promising leads turn up. The meeting ends with assignments: John, Liam, Kathy, and Reggie were among the group assigned to attend the funeral.

Before leaving for the funeral, Liam, John, Kathy, and Reggie corner the profilers. It is their first chance to grab them away from the crowd. This is their case, and they had questions. The six of them grabbed coffee and adjourned to the smaller conference room.

Baker is an average looking guy, clean-cut, short hair, about 40 years old, 6 feet and 175 pounds. He looked like an FBI Agent poster boy. He is married to his college sweetheart and they have three kids, two girls and a boy. His wife is a 'stay at home' mom, at least until the kids are older.

O'Connor, on the other hand, is a 35-year-old who looks like she should be a flight attendant for Aer Lingus, the Irish airline, or on an Ireland tourism poster. She is tall, at least 5-foot-9, very well proportioned, with auburn hair, blue eyes and that Irish 'peaches and cream' complexion. She is a knockout.

The Inspectors ask questions about the profiler's backgrounds, their successes, and their failures. Much to the surprise of the Inspectors, the agents are very frank and honest. A departure from some of their previous encounters with the Federal Government. It turns out Baker has been an agent for 12 years and actually has a degree in Psychology from the University of Chicago. He explains however, that having a degree in Psychology isn't a prerequisite to becoming a profiler; and in fact most of the profilers don't have psychology degrees.

O'Connor, or Mary Ellen as she preferred, has been with the Bureau for six years, but she was a Boston PD officer and Detective for five years before the Bureau. She has worked on a serial killer in Boston and the Bureau was so impressed with her investigative and intuitive talents, that they offered her a job. She had met her husband 'on the job' in Boston, but when she received the Bureau offer, he agreed to resign and move with her to Washington. He immediately signed on with one of the premier Executive Protection firms and they bought a townhouse in Georgetown. She gravitated to the profiling unit and has been there for the past two years. Baker and O'Connor explain that the Behavioral Analysis Unit (BAU), or profiling unit, was originally called the Behavioral Science Unit, however, the Bureau quickly soured on having their prize unit called the BS unit. Hence, the name change.

The two agents assure the Inspectors that there will not be any turf issues. They are there to help and they don't need a press conference… another departure from prior cases. O'Connor, Mary Ellen, went on to say that she hasn't been away from the real police work long enough to forget where her true allegiance lies. The agents explain there were no crystal balls, just the tedious collection of information and the equally tedious process of elimination. They do admit they have the help of some killer software and some extremely fast computers… your tax dollars at work. The meeting ends with handshakes all around.

Back in the garage as the Inspectors get in their cars to attend the funeral, Liam comments that he thought the profilers were OK. There is concurrence among those assembled. Reggie stated he thought agent O'Connor, Mary Ellen, was particularly talented and Liam agreed. Earning him the 'Don't even think about it' look of disapproval from Kathy. Liam immediately backtracked, almost tripping over himself, much to the delight of everyone present.

CHAPTER 26

At the same time, the Chief sits behind his desk, his hands folded in a seemingly relaxed position, while his fingers gripped and flexed, eradicating that illusion. His staff is gathered in his office, along with the Press Information Officers. The office is large, with an executive desk, a conversation grouping in one corner, and a conference table and chairs in the other. Under normal circumstances it is spacious; however, today it is standing room only.

"I think I can safely say that today is going to be a shit storm," he says. "You guys should be prepared for a full court press from the media as soon as the funeral is over. The graveside service will be private, family only, and no media. Once the church is clear, they're going to be all over us for answers. So, let's be ready."

He looks at Melissa Rossi. "Melissa, why don't you check in with Lieutenant Lee? He can brief you on their latest findings. Then, you can coordinate with the other PIOs." He returns his attention to all the people before him. "I'd like for us to be able to give the media the information they need without hindering our investigation. Alright?" Everyone nodded. "Okay, let's get to it."

Later in the morning, news vans for local and national TV and radio stations line the street for blocks by the church. Reporters, cameramen, and sound techs milled around near Saints Peter and Paul Church, but aside from them, the area is eerily still.

With their attention focused on the church, nobody really noticed the SFPD personnel stationed in strategic locations in the park, or on nearby rooftops. Police cameras were filming everything, even if the media wasn't.

At the conclusion of the service, as the doors opened and the congregants poured out into the street, the reporters were all over them. Whether they interviewed family, friends, or acquaintances, it didn't matter; the reporters just hoped to get usable footage or sound bites. Uniformed police officers enforced separation, and the mourners were able to continue on their way, mostly unmolested. The majority filed across the northeast corner of Washington Square and into the Italian Athletic Club, where arrangements had been made for fellowship.

After peeling away from the congregants, John, Liam, Kathy, and Reggie walk toward their cars. "Well, that was horrible," John says with a heavy sigh.

"It sure was," Reggie replies.

Kathy shook her head. "Agreed. No one should have to go through that."

"I don't know how they got through it," Liam says, thinking of the Rosinis. "But you know what'll be even worse? Tonight, when everyone has gone home, and it's just you and your family. You put your other kids to bed, and you see that empty bed and know that your daughter is never coming home again. That would kill me."

John crinkled his forehead. "I know, I just can't imagine."

Kathy took a deep breath and tried to purge the mournful feelings. "I think this is going to be one long day. Does anyone want to grab some lunch before we head back?"

"Yeah," Reggie nods. "That sounds like a sensible idea."

Liam stopped in his tracks. The others turned to see what was wrong. All they saw was excitement in his eyes.

"Lunch!" he exclaims.

"Yeah, we're pretty jazzed about it, too," John says in a deadpan tone.

"Lunch, that's it!" Liam's breathing quickened, his excitement growing as he ignored John's sarcasm. "John, give me the keys. You guys go get some lunch and I'll meet you back at the office."

Liam grabs the keys from John's hand before it is even fully extended, and sprints toward the car, oblivious to the stares of the others. The three inspector's watch as Liam runs to the parked car. Kathy looks at John, shakes her head and comments, "Don't look at me, he's your partner."

The 15-minute drive back to the Hall of Justice seems like forever as Liam chafed at the midday traffic. Once there, he goes directly to the AV Department. "Hey," he says as he breezed in the doors, "can you load up the footage we were looking at this morning from that grocery store on Stockton?"

"Sure," the tech replies, startled by Liam's sudden presence.

Liam resumes his position in front of the monitor as the scene outside the store appeared. He began looking at a week's worth of footage, speeding up through certain times of day, slowing down at others, then backing up to get another look. After a few minutes, he sees a familiar van arrive, then pulls away, with the visor down. As usual.

"Damn!" he spat under his breath.

He continued scrolling through the video and slowing it down again on the second day. Again, he spotted the Harris Painting truck arriving at, and leaving the store, but he could not see the driver.

On the third day before the abduction, the van pulled away from the store… and there it is - the visor is up!

Liam let the moment pass, having expected it to be visor-down, just like the others, and then he had to rewind. When the crucial moment arrived again, Liam freezes the video and stares at it for several moments. He sits forward, looks more closely at the screen, his breathing quickening, his heart pounding.

Suddenly, his excitement burst out. "Got you, you bastard!" he bellows at the monitor. "You had to get something to eat. You finally fucked up!"

Startled for the second time, the AV tech and his partner run to Liam to be sure everything is alright. "Hey," Liam said, "can you blow up and crop the image of this guy's face?"

The techs look at the picture on the screen. It is surprisingly clear; despite being captured through the windshield. "There are a few minor reflections on the glass, but nothing too drastic. Should be easy enough," one says.

"Great! Also, some shots of the van, please. And I need them yesterday."

"We're on it. Give us about 30 minutes."

"I'll wait."

Liam paces back and forth, checking his watch every five minutes. Finally, after 25 minutes that felt like a day, the AV tech returns and hands Liam a manila folder. He also hands Liam a sharp, enhanced photo of the driver, as well as clear shots of the front, rear, and side views of the van.

"Wonderful!" Liam enthused. "I'll be back. Don't go anywhere!"

The lunch rush is over, and the funeral crowd had thinned, which made the drive back to the church a couple of minutes quicker. Liam reaches the front door of the rectory and asks for Monsignor Lombardi. When the Monsignor appears, he smiled in recognition.

"Good afternoon, Inspector. How can I help you?"

"Monsignor, I'd like you to look at a few photos and see
if you can see the man who did the painting here at the
church."

"Certainly. I'd be happy to. Come in."

The Monsignor leads him into a dining room, and Liam
approaches the large dining table. He pulls out six photographs, one of the man in the van, the other five of people who resembled the suspect. He has picked up the other
photos from the Records Section on his way out. He places
them face down on the table.

"Monsignor, I'm going to turn all six of these photos over,
and I'd like you to look at all of them and tell me if you
see the person who identified himself as Chester Wells, the
painter on the church renovation."

"You're saying his picture is in this group?"

"No, Monsignor," Liam said carefully, "I'm not saying his
photo is in the group. I need you to tell me if his photo is
in the group. There are numbers on the back of each of the
photos. If you see the man, please pick up the photo and tell
me the number."

"Okay."

The Monsignor sits down and Liam begins to turn the
photographs over. Monsignor Lombardi picks up the first
one and studies it carefully. Finally, he places it to the right of
the others and begins studying the second one. Liam forces
himself to be patient. He wants the Monsignor to be certain.

When there were five photos in the pile on the right, Liam looks at the Monsignor. He is holding the remaining photo, and nodding.

"This is the man," he said. "Number four."

"Are you sure this is the painter," Liam keeps his voice level, "you personally paid for his work?"

"I'm positive."

"Monsignor, thank you so much. You've been a huge help. Please sign the back of the photo and include today's date."

The Monsignor signs the photo and Liam quickly gathers up the photos and slips them back into the envelope. He says a hasty goodbye to the Monsignor and runs back to the car. His mind racing as he wove through the traffic all the way back to the Hall of Justice.

Once he arrives, his first stop is the AV Department.

"I love you guys!" he gushes. "This is great. We have a description, DNA, and now, thanks to you, a picture. I think this may be the most requested photo you'll ever develop. Can you make me about a dozen copies?"

"We thought you might need a few," the tech said. He hands Liam another envelope, stuffed with papers. "Here's the dozen you want, and an additional dozen. Just catch this asshole."

"Thanks. We will!"

A minute later, Liam rushes into Danny's office. "Lieutenant, I've finally got some good news!"

"Okay," Danny says, unaccustomed to seeing Liam so excited. "Is it for me only? Or are you going to share?"

"It's for you, for starters. Then you can decide exactly how you want to disseminate it."

"Let's have it."

Liam pulled one of the photos out of the envelope and handed it to Danny.

"Gorgeous. Who am I looking at?"

"Our suspect."

Now it is Danny's turn to be startled. "What? How?"

"There's a grocery store on Stockton with a surveillance camera. Every day it captured this asshole leaving at the end of the day with the visor down, blocking his face. The camera at the church got him coming to work with the visor down, no visible image. Today, it hit me that the motherfucker had to eat, and I was hoping he didn't brown bag it. Finally, three days before the abduction, he pulls out at lunchtime, and the visor's up, and that's what he looks like."

"Unbelievable."

"AV gets a huge pat on the back," Liam said magnanimously. "They cropped this from the video surveillance, enhanced it, and added the various views of the van. They are fantastic."

"Let's get some copies made."

"Here's two dozen." Liam hands Danny the envelope.

"Impressive."

"AV again."

"Good work! I think we have enough to call a press conference and give this to the media," Danny says, "but first I have to tell the Chief."

What a relief to finally present the Chief with some good news, Danny thinks as he sums it up. "Without a print or DNA-positive identification, we still don't know who this guy really is. All we have is a name, a van, a photo, and DNA that belongs to someone. Maybe we'll get lucky, and some Good Samaritan will have seen this guy around town, or seen the van, and they'll call us."

Chief Walker nods. "Not to be callous, but if we can get this out to the public today, so it runs with the coverage of the funeral, we'll have the public's undivided attention and hopefully someone will be moved to give up this shithead."

"Yes, sir. Well, it's time for me to go back for our afternoon briefing. If it's okay with you, I'll have these photos distributed to the department, so all the black and whites have them for swing shift today."

"Sounds good," the Chief agrees. "I'll get our PIOs and schedule a press conference for 3 p.m. That gets us on the news at 4, 5, 6, 7, 10 and 11. By the way, where are those Bureau Profilers on this case?"

"They're working their collective asses off. They have a bunch of Bureau people going through and hand searching several cases for something that sounds anything like our case. They've already run the DNA we found through all their databases, but no luck."

"We'll include just how hard they're working, and how much help the Bureau has been, in the press conference," the Chief said.

"I think they definitely deserve a pat on the back."

"Where did you go in such a hurry?" Kathy asks as she returned to Homicide with John and Reggie.

"And why the smug face, or is it more a Cheshire Cat?" John asks.

"Oh, I had to be someplace," Liam replies evasively.

"Okay, give," Kathy says. "What's the big secret?"

"No secret, I just had to go and pick up a photo of our suspect."

"Huh?" John does a double take.

"A photo?" Reggie asks, confused.

"Yup," Liam holds up one of the photos. "Here he is."

Liam's audience looks back at him incredulously. "Wait," John said. "I thought the van surveillance photos all had the visor down. There were no good shots of the driver."

"All very true," Liam agreed. "But then this very clever, very intuitive investigator comes up with the brilliant idea that this devious person of interest probably needs nourishment, just like the rest of us. So, when lunch is mentioned earlier, I had the foresight to rush back to AV and look at the surveillance video again, only this time at noon. And the boy genius got lucky. Three days before the abduction, this asshole forgot to put the visor down." Liam punctuated his narrative by slamming the photo down on his desk.

Kathy smiles. "That's great!"

John looks doubtful. "What's wrong, John?" Reggie asks.

"Well," John glanced at Reggie, then looked back at Liam, "not to rain on your parade, but how do we know he didn't have a helper, and the person we see here is the helper going out for sandwiches?"

"Oh, shit," Reggie turns away from the photo, "that's possible."

"No, it's not," Liam replies, confidently shaking his head as more of the Cheshire Cat came into focus. "I took the liberty of taking this photo along with five other fillers to the good Monsignor, and he picked this asshole out immediately. We have a positive ID."

"Partner, you are a god!" John says, finally allowing himself to feel enthusiastic about the photo.

Kathy puts her arms out and bending at the waist, bowed down to Liam. John and Reggie take up the gesture as well. Liam watches them and smiles, wondering which of them is going to peel a grape for him.

The suspect is on Illinois Street, studying a collection of maps. The missing girl has now morphed into the murdered girl, and he is paying more attention to the local news. As the daughter of a Firefighter, a local Catholic School girl, a good girl with no criminal history, the girl who could be everyone's daughter, she is the lead story on all the channels. Police are pulling out all the stops to identify and apprehend the killer.

As he watches, he decides to begin detailing his departure from San Francisco. His first decision will be the selection of his next destination. To that end, he needs maps.

He looks up the California State Automobile Association (CSAA) office closest to him, and then checks the bus schedules. There is a CSAA office on Sutter Street, near Union Square. He grabs his jacket and walks to the Ferry Building. Once there, he stops for a cup of coffee and a muffin. He sits and watches boats on the Bay while eating his abbreviated breakfast. After he finishes, he grabs a streetcar going west on Market Street, gets off at Powell, and takes the cable car to Union Square.

At the CSAA office, he goes to the trip planning section and waits his turn. When it's his turn, he asks if he can get maps for the Oregon and Idaho areas. The customer service person asks for his membership card. He hadn't thought of that. Again she asks, "Are you a member?"

"No, I'm not, but I only need a couple of maps. I'll gladly pay for them."

"The trip planning and free maps are for members only, but we do have another service for non-members, that may work for you."

"Go ahead, I'm all ears."

'If you'll look behind you in the lobby, you'll see what appears to be a large vending machine."

"I see it."

"Well, it's actually a map vending machine that will dispense maps for two dollars each. I can sell you two-dollar tokens that will operate the vending machine and you can select the maps you need from the directory. Then you just push the corresponding letter and number, and voila, you have your map."

"That's quite ingenious."

He pulls out his wallet and gives the representative a $10 bill and collects his five tokens. He walks to the lobby and the vending machine where he purchases five maps: Oregon, Idaho, Washington, Montana, and Northern California.

With maps in hand, he retraces his route back home and begins the process of selecting both a new destination and the best route to get there. People are just going out of their way to help him escape... and they didn't know it. Even better.

CHAPTER 27

"Okay, quiet down, everyone," Danny says as he stands at the front of the Training Room to start the afternoon briefing. He gives a long, dramatic pause, then continues. "We got a break this morning. We now know what our suspect looks like. A surveillance camera on a grocery store on Stockton caught a photo of his face when he drove off the property to eat lunch."

"Thank God for Big Brother," says somebody in the room.

"Amen. There will be a press conference today at 3 p.m., and the media will be given the photo and an 800 number to call with information. We're going to have to help with the phones on the 800 line." A little groaning spread around the room. "Obviously," Danny continued, "you all know just how crazy these tip lines can become, and you all know that we do occasionally break a case on a tip. So, no bitching, we'll all take our turn."

"So, you think he's still in town?" asks a Missing Persons detective.

"I really don't know, but yes, for now I'd like to believe he's still in town. On the flip side, we've asked the airport police at SFO, Oakland, and San Jose to check their parking lots for the van. We've made the same request of Cal Train, BART, SamTrans, Golden Gate Transit, Muni, and Alameda County Transit. We just don't know, so we're trying to cover all the bases."

"Are we keeping the task force?"

"For now, yes. If this guy is still in town, he must have the van hidden somewhere. Maybe a conscientious landlord will remember the van or the suspect, and then call it in. Maybe someone will recognize him and call it in. Maybe the Bureau and the profilers will get lucky and find the case that will ID our guy and tie him to a shitload of rapes and homicides."

"So, we'll split up into three groups: one goes and gets some rest, one hits the street and checks their sources to see if they can find his hiding place, and the lucky number three, to the phones. We'll alternate on a set schedule. Check it before you leave."

Danny steps away from the podium; everyone knew the meeting was over. They gathered up their things and began dispersing, breaking up into the three assigned groups.

CHAPTER 28

He's decided on Bend, Oregon. The mountain town seems like a nice change of pace, he thinks, as he looks at the open maps in front of him. Maybe he'll sell the remaining van, the one he used to take the girl. He has been extremely careful, so there isn't likely anything in the van to incriminate him. With the van gone, it would completely eliminate the possibility of tying it back to him, and it will provide him a little additional traveling money besides.

There is no rush. He still has two weeks remaining on his lease. Plenty of time to decide what the future held for him.

His thoughts are interrupted by the insistent growling of his stomach. He looks at his watch. It is just about dinner time, and he's had nothing to eat since the muffin that morning. Maybe he'd walk down Potrero Avenue to that little diner on Third Street and get some dinner.

It doesn't take long to get there. Within minutes, he is sitting in a booth, looking at a menu. His attention is drawn to the TV playing over the counter as the news starts. The first story is about the funeral of the schoolgirl from Saints Peter and Paul School. He smiles when they show her picture, remembering his time with her just the other night. Then, he turns his attention back to the menu to satisfy his persistent stomach.

Then his attention is pulled back to the TV, they are showing his picture as part of the report! *How could that be?* He has been so careful! Next, they show photos of his van, followed again by the photo of his face, finally coupled with an 800 number.

Oh my god, this is bad!

He keeps his head down as he stands up and casually walks toward the door, patting his pockets as if he had forgotten his wallet. Once outside, his head remains down as he quickly walks back to his place.

Suddenly, he feels a real sense of urgency. He doesn't have the two weeks he thought, and he needs a Plan B. He forces himself to take a breath. He still has some time. They don't know his name, and they don't know where he or his van are located. His timeline has just advanced quite a bit, but there is no need to panic.

He starts gathering his things and stuffing them in a duffle bag with straps that allow him to carry it on his back. In the morning, he'll get a hat and some sunglasses, and then he takes off.

But what about the van? Suddenly, he felt sleepy, overwhelmed by anxiety. A good night's sleep will help. He'll make a definite decision about the van in the morning.

He pulls the .45 from the shoulder holster, hidden by his jacket. He's carried the gun for years to feel safe all that time. It will help overnight, as well. He places it on the cheap nightstand next to his bed.

Can't be too careful!

"Fourteen-year-old Lucia Rosini was laid to rest yesterday," the anchor says on the morning news. Osborne putters in the kitchen, getting his breakfast, and only half-paying attention. He'd heard about the investigation into the rape and murder, and at the mention of the girl's name, glances at the TV and shakes his head.

"Such a shame," he mutters to himself. "How can someone do something like that?" He goes back to preparing his breakfast as the report continues about Lucia. From there, the newscaster segued into presenting coverage of the police manhunt currently underway for the man who has done the heinous deed.

"If you've seen this man or have any information about his whereabouts, please call the number on your screen."

Osborne glances again at the screen. Something is familiar. He stepped closer to the TV and pulls his glasses from his shirt pocket. He puts on his glasses and tilts his head back as he looked at the face of the killer.

"Oh, my God, that's my tenant!" he exclaimed.

CHAPTER 29

The profilers fully take over the Homicide Conference Room. Folders are strewn across the table, apparently haphazardly, though according to the profilers, there is definitely a system.

Baker and O'Connor have gone through the files for the last couple days, skimming and logging the pertinent information, putting them aside, then opening the next one in the stack. Each of them would sit back periodically, take a deep breath, rotate their heads, and stretch their neck muscles in attempts to stay alert. Then they switched files, a second set of eyes on each file.

Now, finally, they don't need help staying alert. They are both very alert, maybe even a bit manic. Baker has uncovered an old Maryland case that seemed to fit many of the details of the current case. After discussing some of the details with O'Connor, and getting her concurrence, he calls the Maryland Agency to talk to someone familiar with the case.

O'Connor continues her own search, while still listening to Baker's side of the Maryland conversation.

Their supervisor, Clark, comes in just as Baker hangs up the phone. "What's up?" he asks, sensing a certain electricity in the room.

"Well," Baker explains, "We found this case from Maryland, an assault, abduction, and attempted rape, with an identified suspect. But we didn't know, it just struck us as weird. It has all the earmarks of our case, and the report lists DNA as evidence in the trial, but the DNA doesn't match our guy.

"I was able to talk to the arresting agent in Maryland. Turns out this guy grabs a young woman and is attempting to kidnap her when things go bad. She fights like hell. She kicks him in the balls, then she is able to grab a rock and hit him with it. She gets away from him, and goes to the police. Provided with her description of the suspect and his vehicle, they caught him. Later, she is able to positively ID him."

"So, why isn't the DNA on file?" Clark asks. "That would have saved us a lot of work."

"Well, that's where it gets weird, but it finally makes sense now. When she was struggling with him, the young woman cut her hand, and she bled on his clothes. They convicted him with her DNA on his shirt. His DNA is taken at his booking, but it isn't used at trial. With all the other evidence, her DNA on his clothes, and the positive ID, his DNA is placed in evidence, but not the system."

"So, he's been in the system," O'Connor says, "but without his DNA. And without the DNA, he's been untouchable."

"That about sums it up."

Baker hears a ping on his laptop. He turns to it, opening his email program.

"Unbelievable," Clark says. "So, who is this asshole?"

Baker turns his computer toward Clark and O'Connor. Their suspect stares back from his old booking photo. He is younger, but it is definitely him.

"Jed Wilson," Baker said, "originally from Georgia, Less Than Honorable Discharge from the Army, suspect in some sexual assaults where he was stationed, loner, handyman, no real family, no ties. Forty-six years old. He does the full nickel on the Maryland beef, so he is discharged from prison without a parole tail."

"And he's been on the move ever since," O'Connor says.

"Looks that way. I have a feeling he's going to be good for a bunch of these unsolved rape/murders. I've asked the state lab in Maryland to send the DNA to our lab in Quantico, and I've requested an expedited analysis."

"Good." Clark continues. "Not your fault he isn't in the system. Your profile is right on the money, though," he says to both of them.

"Thank you, sir," O'Connor replies for both of them.

"Now, let's see how many of these unsolved cases you can move into the 'solved' column.

Get the rest of the team in here, and let's get as many of these reviewed as we can while we're here. Who knows? SFPD may grab this guy and we'll get a chance to interview him. He's probably looking at capital murder, so he just might be talkative."

"Yes, sir," Baker said.

"And print out a copy of the picture for me. I need to go see the Lieutenant."

A few minutes later, Clark is sitting in front of Danny's desk, filling him in on the latest developments and the Maryland case.

"Un-fucking-believable!" Danny retorts.

"That's the *Reader's Digest* summary. I'll have the complete report for you in about an hour."

"I have to go and fill my Chief in on this latest development," Danny says. "And I'm sure your SAC has a bunch of questions, too."

"I haven't told him yet. I thought you should be the first to know."

"Thank you," Danny says sincerely. "I take back all the bad things I've ever said about the FBI."

"All of them?"

"Well, most."

A crooked grin briefly cracks Clark's stoic demeanor. "I do have a favor to ask," he said, getting back to business.

"Name it."

"When you catch this guy, will you allow my team the opportunity to sit in on the initial interview, and then to interview him separately once you're done?"

"No problem on the interview once we're done," Danny replied. "I'll check with the handling team and see if they have any issues with the team sitting in. I don't think they will."

Clark nods. "Thanks. Well, I'm off to inform my superiors."

"Same here. And thank *you*."

Melissa Rossi and another Press Information Officer have just arrived in the Chief's office to find Danny, for the second time, talking about the latest findings of the profilers.

"So," Chief Walker concludes, "we'd like to call a press conference, to get this latest development out to the public."

Rossi glanced at the other PIOs, then back to the Chief. Doubt is showing on her face.

"Chief," she says, "we just had a major conference yesterday afternoon. I think a second one, this soon, would not be as valuable." The Chief sits back in his chair as Rossi speaks, mulling over this new contradictory thought. Rossi continues, "We've talked about this, and we think the next press conference should be you, the Lieutenant, and the Bureau announcing the apprehension of the suspect." She includes a glance at Danny. "The perfect example of law enforcement cooperation leading to the apprehension of a dangerous rapist/murderer."

"But, what about this new information?" the Chief asks. "It's critical that it gets out to the public. Someone may know this guy and maybe even knows where he might be heading."

"Chief," another PIO speaks up, "we call the networks and they run a banner under whatever show that's currently playing. Or maybe they do the full screen 'Breaking News,' and they cut to a reporter who makes the announcement."

Rossi nods her agreement.

"It's dramatic," the PIO says, "and it gets the information out to the public. It says we're too busy trying to find this guy, and don't have time for press conferences."

"Hmm," the Chief mulls this over. After a couple of moments, he agrees. "Okay, we'll do it your way. Go ahead and set it in motion."

"Yes, sir," they say in stereo.

After they file out of the office, Chief Walker looks at Danny. "I remember when they were police officers, and not PR and political people."

"Yeah, I know," Danny replies. "They're good, though. And they had the balls to tell you that you might be wrong."

"Wrong?" The Chief looks at Danny, his eyebrows raised.

"Or, perhaps, just not the 'rightest' you've ever been," Danny says with a smile.

"We'll just call it an alternative direction."

"If you say so, sir."

"Of course, we'll never know now."

The Chief leans forward and looks at the mug shot on his desk. Then he turns his attention back to Danny. "Great work on this case, Lieutenant. You and your team have done a tremendous job. And you've even managed to play nice with the Bureau."

"The Bureau is a huge help, and they've been a real ally. I may have to rethink my original position."

"Now, don't go all Kumbaya on me. Remember the frog and the scorpion."

Danny laughed. "Yes, sir."

CHAPTER 30

There is a drone of voices, punctuated by an occasional ringing phone, as Danny enters the Tip Line telephone room. He walks to the desk where the supervising inspector, Leslie Kenrick, is seated. She stands up as he approaches, but Danny waves her back to her chair.

"How's it going?" Danny asks.

"About as you'd expect, Lieutenant," Kenrick replies. "The third shift has just come on, and the phones are still ringing, but not as often as last night."

"Has anything worthwhile come from it?"

"Oh, lots." Kenrick picks up a stack of forms and begins leafing through them. "Let's see, he was sighted at: Ocean Beach, Mt. Davidson, Twin Peaks, crossing the Golden Gate, at a Giants game, at a Warriors game, walking on Market Street, and a host of others. The tips that seem most current get an immediate patrol response, and the rest are being filed."

197

"Okay, so no real leads?"

"Not so far," she says, putting down those papers and picking up a different collection. "Not unless you want to go to this Psychic Hotline stack. In that case, we know for sure: he's by a body of water, he's a foreign transplant, he's a Russian spy, he's a polygamist looking for wives, he's in Las Vegas, and a few others. Honestly, if this weren't so serious, we should record these screwballs and play the collection online for a fee."

Danny laughed at the thought.

Kenrick's attention is drawn away as one of the inspectors on the phone lines waves her over. Danny follows her.

"Boss," the inspector says, "I just talked to a guy, one that actually gave me a call back number that works, and he claims he rented a building with a storage lot to a guy that is a dead ringer for our suspect. He went on to say the guy said he is a painter, and he has an older van."

"Anything else?" Kenrick asks.

"He says the rent is paid up for another two weeks, and he thinks the guy may still be there. And best of all, he has keys to the lock on the gate, and to the building."

Kenrick turns to Danny. "What do you think?"

"I think we need to talk to this guy in person and get an address for his property."

"I've got the address," the inspector says, handing Danny a sheet of paper.

When he returns to the Homicide Bureau, Danny sees Liam, John, Kathy, and Reggie at their desks. They all look up as he walks toward them, seeing a sense of purpose in his approach.

"We have a guy on the Tip Line that sounds legit," Danny says. "He claims he rented a building with a surrounding lot to a guy with an older van. The van logo and the guy himself said he was a painter and, best of all, the caller gives a positive ID of the suspect from the photo on TV."

"I love it when things start coming together," Liam says.

"What do you want us to do?" Kathy asks.

"You and Reggie go interview this caller and size him up. See if he's got all his marbles, and collect the keys to the property from him. Danny hands John the address. "John, you and Liam go to the property in Potrero Hill and sit on it. See if there's any activity, and if it matches the description given by our caller. I'll contact our Assistant District Attorney and have him start drawing up a search warrant and getting a Judge on standby. Once you've seen the property, call me so I can include an accurate description in the affidavit."

"Got it," John replies.

The four gather up their things and head to their respective assignments.

The long guitar jam that made up the second half of the Allman Brothers' 'Ramblin' Man', is playing on the little radio as the suspect packed his belongings. The duffle bag with the shoulder straps is completely packed and lying on the floor by the door. His .45 is loaded and comfortably secured in his shoulder holster. He just needs to decide what to do about the van.

The guitars fade out as an announcer comes on the radio:

"Breaking News. SFPD and the FBI just announced a break in the Lucia Rosini murder. Police have identified the previously unknown suspect as Jed Wilson from Georgia. Additionally, he may be going by the alias of Chester Wells. Wilson is a white male, 5'11", 175 pounds, with brown hair and eyes. He was last seen driving an older model van, with a 'Harris Painting' logo on the side. Anyone with information on this man should call the SFPD Tip Line at 800-CATCH-ME, or 800-228-2463."

Jed stared dumbly at the radio as 'Hold on Loosely' by another Georgia classic rock band, '.38 Special', began playing. Finally, he musters up the strength to reach for the radio and turn it off.

"Shit!" he shouts. "How did they ID me?"

He begins pacing like a newly caged wild animal as he ruminates out loud on his time in San Francisco. "I was so careful. There are no prints, no witnesses. I didn't use valid plates or ID. I didn't leave DNA, or a paper trail, I used cash only. Dammit! What went wrong?"

He shakes his head. It doesn't matter now. He'll figure it out later. For now, he has to get away.

He scans the building, his mind racing, as if the building holds the secret to his escape. He knows the airports and train stations will be crawling with cops looking for him. They will know he'll want to make a fast getaway, so he'll have to settle for a slower one. Nobody bothers to check IDs on a bus. He'll catch a local bus to the Greyhound depot, then take the bus out of town. He'll be a little short on cash since the van sale is off the table, but that is the hand he's been dealt.

He takes a deep breath, feeling relief wash over him, now knowing he has a plan. But before he leaves, he needs to go over the building with a fine-toothed comb. He needs to eliminate any trace of evidence pointing to him and clean the place from top to bottom.

But why bother? He realizes they know who he is. They had his photo – but he still can't figure out how they got it. They know he is here, so cleaning the building and the van wouldn't eliminate that evidence, besides, it will take too much time.

The best Plan B's usually involve fire. DNA and prints can't survive fire, and God knows he has enough flammable liquid in the van to do the job.

He begins to move with purpose. He has a plan, and that gives him confidence. He pulls a couple of five-gallon buckets of paint thinner from the van and pours it around the building, starting in the living area. Once he is back in the garage portion, he pours thinner around the perimeter, occasionally splashing it on the walls. Then, he takes the remaining liquid and splashes it inside the van.

He hates to burn the van. He'd hoped to make his escape in the painting van, but that isn't an option now. He takes his bag outside and places it next to the open gate. Everything has to be ready. A running man draws attention. He wants to be able to walk out calmly.

Taking a last look around, he grabs an empty potato chip bag out of the trash. He flattens it out and places it on top of a puddle of paint thinner. He pulls a pack of Winston's from his shirt pocket and removes a cigarette. He places the cigarette in his mouth and prepares to light it. This is the crucial part, surrounded as he is by flammable liquid. He squats down and lights the cigarette. He pinches the cigarette between his thumb and forefinger and carefully props it up on the potato chip bag.

Once the cigarette burns down, it will ignite the waxy coating on the chip bag, which will then ignite the paint thinner. The fire will follow the paths of flammable liquid and spread throughout the building in seconds. Spontaneous combustion, no trace of evidence. His time spent in conversation with a serial arsonist in that Maryland prison hasn't been wasted.

He stands up, knowing he has about three and a half minutes of cigarette burn time to get away. He walks out the door, picks up his bag at the gate, and begins his walk down Illinois Street.

"He seemed like a nice enough fellow," Osborne said, "and he paid cash. That property is tough to rent as it's just not that valuable yet."

"I think it will be," Kathy said, "what with the Giants and the Warriors in the area."

"That's what they tell me. I just have to hold on. Well, this fellow's rent is helping with that holding on."

Kathy fans out a selection of photographs in front of Osborne. She knows this is redundant as Osborne has already seen the suspect's photo on TV, but she is determined to cross all the t's and dot all the i's.

"Is your tenant one of these men?"

"Yes, that's him." He immediately points to the picture of Jed Wilson.

"Mr. Osborne," Reggie said, "you told the inspector on the phone that you have the keys to the Illinois Street property."

Osborne nods. "That's right."

"Could we have them? And do we have your permission to enter the property?"

"You sure do." Osborne hands the keys to Reggie. "Such a shame about that poor girl."

"Thank you, sir," Reggie says.

Kathy turns to Osborne as they prepare to leave. "We'll be in touch, Mr. Osborne."

She calls Lieutenant Lee as they get in the car. "Well, Lieutenant," she says when Danny answers, "he's the real deal. Picks out our guy in the photo array, describes the van to a T, and confirms the guy is paid up for two more weeks."

"Thanks," Danny replies. "I'll get this to Hernandez for the warrant. Why don't you head over that way and standby until I can get the warrant? John and Liam should be there about now."

"Roger that."

"And I don't know if this guy can monitor us, so don't use the radio. Let's use the phone for any future correspondence."

"Got it."

CHAPTER 31

A column of smoke billows ahead of John and Liam as they arrive in the neighborhood of the rented property.

"Is that a building fire?" John asks.

"Sure looks like it," Liam replies, "and it looks big. I'll call Fire."

He picks up the radio and thumbed the button on the mic. "Dispatch, we have a large structure fire east of Third Street and south of 20th. When we get closer, I can give you an exact address."

"Be advised," the dispatcher replies, "Fire is responding to a structure fire in the 900 block of Illinois."

"That would be the one," Liam says, replacing the mic.

"Wait—" John said. "Aren't we supposed to be watching a building in the 900 block of Illinois?"

Liam picks up the paper with the address on it. "You're right. We might as well just drive up. There's no element of surprise left for this one."

"Better get the Lieutenant on the phone."

Liam is already reaching for his phone as they pull up and park near the building. After Danny picks up, he says, "Lieutenant, thought you would want to know, the building in question seems to be going up in smoke."

"What?" Danny asks, alarmed.

"I'm guessing he's torched it."

"That's just great," Danny says. "Okay, I'll continue with the warrant, just in case. Can you see if there's any way you can get Fire to try and not destroy everything in the building?"

"We can try, but this thing's really burning. I think they're going to be busy just putting the fire out. Besides, I don't think anything of evidentiary value is going to make it."

"See if they can determine if the van is still in the building. Maybe our guy is on foot. We may still have a chance."

"Kathy and Reggie should be there shortly. I'll get the information out to Patrol, just in case our boy is on foot in the area."

"On the way," Liam says as he gets out of the car.

Liam disconnects and slips his phone back in its holster on his belt. The Fire Captain is busy directing his firefighters as Liam approaches.

"Captain," he shouts over the bedlam, "Any chance you could get someone close enough to see if there's a van inside the building? It's an important piece of evidence."

"Are you out of your mind?" The Captain looks at him as if he knew the answer. "It's way too hot and too dangerous.

I'm not risking one of my people for a piece of potential evidence."

"Okay, let's try this, do you think you might feel differently if I told you the potential piece of evidence could convict the asshole that killed your firefighter's daughter?"

The Captain turns and looks Liam square in the face. "Well, why didn't you say so?"

He turns and begins shouting orders into his radio, directing multiple streams of water toward the front of the building. After a few minutes of the intensified assault, one firefighter is able to get close to the doorway. The metal overhead garage door is badly distorted by the heat, but still in place, for the most part. The wooden entry door next to it, though, is burned to a crisp, and the high-pressure streams of water have knocked the charred wood down, opening the doorway. Through the opening, illuminated by the blaze within, the firefighter is able to get a glimpse inside.

Liam watched as the Captain listened to his radio for a moment, before coming toward him.

"Inspector," he reports, "there's a van in the building. It looks like the one you want. Still too hot to get inside, though, and I'm afraid the roof will come down. I've got to pull my people back."

"Don't risk anyone," Liam says. "The info on the van is great. Thank you."

Liam immediately has Danny back on the phone. "Lieutenant, the van is in the building."

"You're sure?"

"Yes. Fire is able to look inside the building."

Liam goes on. "I wonder why he left his 'murder' vehicle behind; maybe he has another vehicle to drive out of town."

"Could be. He's careful. I guess that's why he's been on the loose for so long. I'll get this out to Patrol." Danny hangs up.

Jed watched the activity from a safe distance until the 'S' Shuttle bus arrived and he climbed on board. Police and fire personnel are all over the place, but he felt safe. They are focused on the fire. They don't notice him.

He places the big duffle bag on the seat next to him and relaxes. He is almost there. Just a few minutes, a relatively short ride north, and he'll be out of there. He still has to walk a few blocks to the Greyhound station, but he knows there is a Giants game. The increased foot traffic in the area will help. There is anonymity in crowds.

As the bus approaches the Folsom Street stop, he stands and wrestles the bag up onto his shoulders. He steps down off the bus and starts walking.

"So, what do you think?" Liam asks Kathy and Reggie, who have just arrived. They are discussing their options.

"I think he's still in the area," John says.

"What if he set the fire with a timer and left last night?" Liam wonders.

"I don't think so," John replies. "If he left last night, I think he would have set the timer closer to that time, to provide cover for his escape."

"I think he's still here too," Kathy says.

"I'm with you guys," Reggie says. "I have a feeling he's still nearby."

"Okay," Liam nods, "I'm in. Let's get a patrol car to stand-by at the fire scene while we go look for this guy."

"Where do you think he'd go?" John asks.

"There's a Giants game today." Liam offers, "So, there's a crowd to get lost in around the Ballpark."

"And there's the Greyhound Terminal," Kathy adds. "Not much security or surveillance there."

"Cal Train is just up the block," John says, "but their security is pretty tight."

"Alright," Liam concludes, "let's head up to the ballpark and Greyhound. They seem the most logical."

"We'll take the ballpark crowd," John says.

"Okay," Kathy adds. "Reggie and I will take Greyhound."

CHAPTER 32

It won't be long now. Jed walks southwest on Folsom, away from the Embarcadero, the Greyhound Terminal just a couple of blocks ahead, past the twisting, turning façade of the Folsom Tower.

He feels confident. Freedom is within reach. As expected, traffic is heavy, both on the street and the sidewalk. Today, that is fine with him. He is just another faceless person, lost in the city maze.

But not quite faceless. His face has been all over the news. He thinks it's prudent to keep his head down, only glancing up and around periodically to keep his bearings. Therefore, he doesn't see the SFPD motorcycle officers until he is almost directly across the street from them. They are leaning against their bikes as they monitor the heavy afternoon traffic, relaxed but alert.

Alert enough that they noticed him.

Jed thinks he sees recognition flash across their faces. Fighting the panic, he looks ahead, his eyes darting back and forth.

Keep it together, he tells himself. Just keep walking. You don't know that they recognized you. His chest pounds and his heart pumps from the adrenalin suddenly flooding his system. It is all he could do to stay cool.

Then he can't help himself. He glances across the street again — and they are watching him. Their relaxed posture is gone. One is already climbing on his motorcycle. The other is still watching, and it looked like he may be reaching for his sidearm.

Jed can't take it anymore, not when freedom is this close. He pulls out his .45 and opens fire. The cop on the motorcycle goes down, but the other one dives behind a parked car.

The crowd suddenly evaporates, with some bystanders screaming. There is traffic in the street, so when the cop draws his gun and looks around the parked car, he can't fire. Another thing crowds are good for – innocent bystanders.

He doesn't realize how many shots he has fired until the hammer connects with a click - empty magazine, and an unloaded gun. He has another magazine in his jacket pocket, and he quickly reloads. He fires one more shot to make the cop take cover. Then, he takes off running, as fast as he can. But the light is red and the one-way traffic crossing on Spear is heavy. He can't get across, and he can't just stand on the corner waiting. He turns to the left, running down Spear.

He doesn't like it, though. He is running away from his destination. He'll have to go around the block and head back toward Folsom, then he'll arrive at the bus station. But first, he has to get across Spear.

"Shots fired," the call comes over the radio. "Officer down on Folsom Street, west of the Embarcadero. Suspect is a white male with a large duffle bag, last seen on Spear, running toward Harrison. We need paramedics and an ambulance to this location."

"That's just up the street!" John says, as he and Liam keep their eyes peeled for their suspect.

John points. "There he is!"

Liam thumbed the button on the radio. "Suspect sighted on Harrison, turning north, now on Main, heading toward the bus station."

John accelerates up the street, in hope of cutting him off. Weighed down with the duffle bag on his back, Jed seems to be tiring out. Just as John and Liam are coming alongside him, Jed looked over his shoulder toward them.

"He's seen us," Liam says.

Jed stops and allows the bag to drop from his shoulders. As the car skids in a turn to stop in front of him, he lifts his gun and fires toward them. John and Liam pull their guns and jump from the car, using the open doors as cover. Liam hears a bullet thud into the fender in front of him.

"Shit."

There were still people in the street, a few frozen in panic, others running different directions to try to stay out of the

212

path of stray bullets, so neither John nor Liam can return fire. But when they heard the telltale sound of an empty gun, they both jump out from behind the car doors, running toward Jed.

Jed's out of ammo, then he sees them coming toward him, he turns and runs, runs away from the bus station. He turns back onto Harrison, but John and Liam are close behind. As soon as they rounded the corner, Jed seems to hear their footsteps gaining on him, and he throws a glance over his shoulder.

Panicking, he runs across Harrison, directly into the path of a car with an Uber sticker in the windshield. The driver is looking down and doesn't see him. The car hits Jed in the legs, crumpling him onto the hood and against the windshield. At 35 miles an hour, the car continues lurching forward for a bit as Jed rolled up over the roof and landed on the street like a rag doll.

When the car finally comes to a stop, it sits there for a moment before speeding off.

Liam lifts his hand held radio. "We have a man down, auto-ped accident. We need paramedics and a Traffic Investigation Unit. The suspect is a dark gray Toyota Camry, on Harrison, with an Uber sticker in the windshield, right front damage."

"That Uber car should be on top of us right about now," Kathy says.

"There he is," Reggie points, "front end smashed. Light him up."

Kathy turns on the emergency lights and chirps the siren at him. The car slows down but keeps moving. When several other police units converged on him, he finally stops.

The sight of police officers pointing guns at him is enough to make the driver put his hands up in surrender.

Jed Wilson, AKA Chester Wells, is strapped to a gurney, his limbs immobilized in splints. Not that he could have moved anyway. Barely alive, he hasn't regained consciousness since the impact.

"What do you say I tell these firefighter paramedics just who their patient is?" Liam asks John. "What do you think this asshole's odds are of surviving the ride to the hospital?"

John raises his eyebrows as he watches the paramedics roll the gurney into the ambulance. "As much as I'd like to kill the bastard myself, I think maybe you'd better ride in the ambulance, just in case they figure it out."

"Okay," Liam grudgingly moves toward the ambulance.

"I know," John says, acknowledging their shared feeling about the man. "I'll follow in the car, and I'll call the Lieutenant."

Liam climbs in and John turns to head back to the car. He shakes his head when he sees the bullet hole in the passenger side fender.

"The suspect shot at two motor cops and hit one," John tells Danny on the phone. "He's alive and enroute to San Francisco General. We found the asshole about a block away and began to chase him. He fired on us and ran across Harrison, head down, right into the path of a car. He's pretty screwed up. Liam is in the ambulance just in case he regains consciousness and makes a statement, and to keep him alive if the paramedics figure out who he is."

"Well, it looks like everybody's going to San Francisco General," Danny replies. "Give me an update as soon as you get there. What about the car that hit the suspect?"

"It only gets better." John chuckles. "The driver took off, an Uber car, and he is ultimately apprehended a few blocks away by Kathy, Reggie, and a bunch of black and whites. He's in custody for felony hit and run."

"God, you can't make this shit up. Good work. I'll tell the Chief."

Melissa Rossi and another PIO are already in Chief Walker's office when Danny gets there. He joins them in waiting as the Chief finished up with a phone call.

"Sir," Rossi says as soon as he hangs up, her voice sounding ragged and tired, "the press is hounding us. They know there was some kind of major activity out there this afternoon, and they want to know if it had anything to do with the Lucia Rosini murder."

The Chief, standing behind his chair, raises his eyebrows, and motions toward Danny as if giving him the floor.

"Go ahead, Lieutenant."

"It did indeed have to do with the murder," Danny replies. "I'm happy to report that we have the suspect in custody. He attempted to evade our officers. Shots were fired and one motorcycle officer was hit. I'm still awaiting word on his condition. Inspectors O'Neill and

Donnelly caught up with the suspect and gave chase, the suspect ran into the path of an Uber driver who wasn't watching the road. He's currently at San Francisco General, unconscious and, apparently, in pretty serious condition."

"Are we certain it's the murderer?" Rossi asked.

"We are certain that it's Jed Wilson," Danny answers carefully, knowing that, legally, Wilson is still just a suspect, an alleged murderer. "From the other evidence and testimony, we've gathered in our investigation, we are reasonably certain that he is the murderer."

"Excellent work, Lieutenant," Chief Walker says. He turns toward the PIOs. "You have enough information to feed to the press for now. We'll make a formal statement when we have all the information."

"Yes, sir," the PIOs say in unison. They acknowledge Danny as they open the door and leave.

"I'm glad you came around," the Chief says. "Your timing is perfect."

"Yes, sir," Danny replies.

"I just got off the phone with the Fire Chief as you came in. He wants to be present when your Inspectors call on the Rosinis."

"Good idea."

The Chief sighs and looks at the paperwork that covers his desk. "Now, unless there's anything else, I still have a shitload of phone calls to make."

"Of course, sir," Danny smiles and leaves the Chief's office.

Danny has just gotten back to his office when his phone rings. It's John.

"John, how goes it?"

"Well, Lieutenant, first of all, our motor cop is going to be okay. He was hit twice. The first is in the upper left arm, through and through, no bone involvement. The second one hit him right in the vest. He'll be sore, but he should be back on the job in no time."

"That's good news. What about our suspect?"

"Not so good for him," John replies. "That car broke both his legs, and his ensuing short flight, culminating with his head hitting the street, didn't do him any good either. The docs say the next 24 hours will tell a great deal."

"Okay. You stay with the suspect until I get you some relief. It won't take long. I'm guessing Kathy and Reggie are involved with the hit and run arrest."

"Yes, sir, I believe so."

"I'm going to have two other Inspectors pick up the Fire Chief and take him to the Rosini's to let them know the person who hurt and killed their daughter won't hurt anyone again."

"I think the family will appreciate that."

"I'll see you when you get back, John. Keep me posted if there are any changes."

"Will do, sir."

"I didn't mean to run away," said Jaron, the Uber driver, as Kathy and Reggie were booking him.

He spoke with a bit of an accent. "But I have no insurance. I will get in big trouble from Uber. They say I must have insurance."

"I can assure you," Kathy says, "you'll be in a lot more trouble if the victim dies."

Jaron's eyes opened wide, and he shook his head. "That man I hit? He come from out of nowhere. He never look; he just ran in front of my car."

"What about the witnesses who saw you on your phone when you hit him?"

"I was just checking the name and address of my next fare. I was not texting or talking."

"You were just reading," Kathy says.

"Yes, yes," he nods vigorously, "just reading."

"Okay," Kathy says, unmoved, "this officer is going to show you to a cell. You'll be given an opportunity to post bail, but if you can't afford insurance, I have a feeling bail will be out of the question, too."

CHAPTER 33

The large Training Room is nearly full, with all of the task force members, including the FBI agents. The mood is considerably more lighthearted than it had been all week. The last to arrive are Danny, Chief Walker, Fire Chief Cavaglieri, and SAC Newell. Danny stands at the podium at the front of the room, and everyone quiets down.

Danny turns to the two Chiefs and the SAC. "Chiefs," he says, "do either of you want to say a few words?"

"No," Chief Walker says, waving his hand. "We think we'll wait until you're done."

"Okay. SAC Newell, do you want the floor?"

"No, thanks. I think I'll wait as well."

"Okay," Danny says, addressing the personnel gathered in front of him. "This has been an incredible week. I want to thank each of you for the outstanding job you did on this case. I know the pay sheets won't reflect even a percentage of the time spent and time donated. To the Bureau Agents and the Profilers, thank you for all your help. As hard as this is to say, we couldn't have done it without you."

The FBI agents smiled at the admission.

"I'm going to ask that a couple of our inspectors brief everyone on the case as it stands this morning. John, let's start with you."

"Okay." John stands up. "Our suspect is still hanging on. They drilled some holes in his head to relieve the pressure, but it's still touch and go. The .45 he used to shoot our motor officer is stolen, taken three years ago in Kansas. In the same city, it turns out, as a reported abduction, rape, and murder. His duffle bag didn't yield anything significant, just some maps of Oregon, Washington, Idaho, Montana and Northern California, with the Bend, Oregon, area highlighted. We assume that's where he was planning on going next."

As he finished and sat down, Reggie stands up.

"We went through the burned building with the Fire Arson Team. The van isn't stolen, nor is it registered. There are several sets of stolen and out-of-date plates for the van in the building. It looks like the van is a salvage build.

"The area that would have been the living area in the building is also burned beyond being of any evidentiary use. Fire is still not sure of the source, but they did locate the point of origin, on the floor just outside the living area. The age of the building, coupled with the flammables in the van, made it a difficult fire to put out."

Reggie sits down, and then Kathy takes over.

"This is one you're going to want to write down," she says with a smile. "Our suspect ran from Inspectors O'Neill and Donnelly. However, if the suspect had only waited a minute and really sized up the opposition, a brisk walk probably would have been enough."

John and Liam looked at each other, shaking their heads. The rest of Kathy's audience thought her joke was much funnier than they did. After the laughter died down, Kathy continues.

"Our bad guy ran right in front of an Uber car being driven by an uninsured driver who was, admittedly, on his phone at the time of the accident. This can only get better. The Uber driver, according to him, then fled the scene because of his lack of insurance. After he was booked, it turns out that he had another reason to run. He's a paroled, convicted, registered rapist, and he knew he was dead once we had him in custody. Well, he's going to stand trial here for either hit and run or vehicular homicide, and then the California Department of Corrections will violate him, and he'll go back for the balance of the original sentence."

"How did he get past the Uber background check?" an erstwhile Narcotics agent asked.

"What background check?" John answers. "If you have a cell phone and a car, you're an Uber driver."

"Too true, unfortunately," Kathy said. "Uber says they don't know how this happened, and they'll be reviewing their background procedures. If anyone has any 'follow home rapes,' since that was our driver's MO, go get him."

Kathy sat down and gestures to Danny.

"Okay, that sums up the week's events," Danny says. "I know several of you will still be writing on this for a few days, so go ahead and get started. Chief, the floor is yours."

Chief Walker and SAC Newell approach the podium.

"I'd just like to congratulate all of you," the Chief says. "You've done a wonderful job on a difficult case, further complicated by having to work with what some of you may think of as the enemy." There is some subdued laughter from both Police and FBI personnel. "So, thank you to the Bureau." He turns to Newell standing next to him, extends his hand and the two shake hands. "As Lieutenant Lee said, we couldn't have done it without you."

"Thank you, Chief Walker," Newell says with a genuine grin. "I know what a difficult admission that was." He turns toward the officers and agents in the room. "And thank you for all your hard work, and your interagency cooperation. This really is a true joint effort and, speaking for all the Bureau staff present, we're glad we could help."

There is scattered applause, and Chief Walker raises his hands to quiet them down.

"We're not done yet," he says, "but almost. Fire Chief Cavaglieri is visiting us and wants to say a few words."

The Fire Chief acknowledges Chief Walker and steps to the podium. Chief Walker and SAC Newell were fairly tall men, each 6 feet or better, but they were rendered insignificant when Chief Cavaglieri approached the podium. He is at least 6-foot-6 and had to go 245 pounds.

"I want to thank all of you," he says warmly. "Losing a child is just beyond comprehension and I hope none of us ever has to go through that experience. You all handled this case from day one like Lucia was one of yours. You protected the family, and you worked your collective asses off to solve this horrible tragedy. On behalf of the Fire Department, thank you from the bottom of our hearts.

"Now, on to another matter. I've spoken to the Chief and SAC Newell, and they both assured me you all have accrued enough compensatory time to take the afternoon off. So, the San Francisco Fire Department would like each of you to be our guests for lunch and a beverage of your choice at the Italian Athletic Club."

The room erupts in cheers and applause. Chief Cavaglieri smiles at everyone as Danny comes to the podium. He shakes Chief Cavaglieri's hand, then turns to the room.

"Dismissed. Get the hell out of here."

A celebratory mood engulfs everyone. The officers and agents, visiting with new friends they made during the investigation, don't seem overly anxious to leave the room.

Shortly afterward, John, Kathy, and Reggie are gathered in Danny's office, along with Assistant District Attorney Hernandez and Profiler Supervisor Clark.

"Where's Liam?" Danny asked.

"He said he had to make a stop in Forensics," John replied. "Said he'd be right up."

"Okay, we'll go ahead and start. I don't want to keep you long. The Fire Department is calling from the IAC wondering where we are, but you need to hear this. Our ADA has some interesting legal issues you need to be aware of, and airing them at the general meeting seemed counterproductive."

Liam comes rushing into the office, holding a file folder, and he sits down in the last available chair. "Sorry I'm late boss," he says.

"No problem. Hernandez is just going to give us a quick summary of the case preparation, if it goes forward."

John sits up. "What do you mean IF?"

"First," Hernandez starts, "I've been on this case since day one, and you've all done an amazing job. I believe, if he lives, we will convict him on the evidence we have. But I just want you to be aware that the defense will attack the DNA evidence you recovered on the plastic bag."

"The bag that contained the victim's body?" Kathy asked.

Hernandez nods, now with an expression that almost looked like embarrassment on his face.

"What's the problem?"

"I believe the defense will claim that the suspect cut his hand and that he handled that bag with his cut hand. Then someone else used that bag to transport the victim. The blood isn't on the victim herself."

"I can't believe it," Kathy says, her ire rising. "Do you think a jury will really entertain that load of crap?"

"Stranger things have happened."

Kathy is seething, if her facial expression is any indication.

Liam has been strangely quiet since sitting down. Finally, he looks up.

"So," Liam says, "what you need is the suspect's DNA on the victim in such a way that only he could have placed it there."

"I'm afraid so," Hernandez says. "I still think we have enough, but I think you need to know about that one possible glitch."

Liam, enjoying the spotlight as he did, stood up for emphasis. "Mr. Hernandez, the reason I'm late to this meeting has to do with a detour through Forensics, where I picked up this document."

"What is it?"

"Patience," Liam replies with a quiet, and unusually soothing tone. "I know we're all aware that the suspect punched Lucia and tore his glove, and that's where we got his DNA on the bag. Well, I went back to Forensics and had them re-examine that piece of latex we found snagged on Lucia's tooth. And ladies and gentlemen, that piece of latex, found in the victim's mouth, contained the blood DNA of our suspect. Mr. Assistant District Attorney Hernandez, I present you with your smoking gun."

One could have heard the proverbial pin drop for several seconds, as the others looked at Liam, stunned. Liam glances from one face to another, thinking that, perhaps, he hasn't made the point clearly enough.

Suddenly, Kathy jumps to her feet and runs into Liam's arms, the force of the collision nearly toppling him backwards into his chair. "Liam Donnelly, I love you!" she yells happily.

The others look at each other, not sure what to do or say. Finally, Kathy lets go of a very startled Liam and steps back from him. Hernandez then rises and approaches Liam, throwing his arms around him. "I love you too, man," he says.

"Okay, I can't take any more of this," Danny says, rising from his desk. "Meeting adjourned to the IAC."

CHAPTER 34

The 'meeting' at the San Francisco Italian American Club continues well into the late night, with the SFIAC kitchen providing traditional dishes that were consumed as soon as they were placed on the tables. The two bars were also doing a land office business with the combination of Police, Fire, and FBI personnel seemingly trying to outdo one another in the alcohol consumption department. Chiefs Walker and Cavaglieri are meeting with Lorenzo in his office, where Lorenzo has adopted, what the Chiefs feel, is an unreasonable position as far as payment is concerned.

"Lucia is from the neighborhood," he says. "She is family. Her father is a firefighter and a member of the SFIAC. He's your family and our family, so you are our family tonight. You don't charge family for food and drink." Lorenzo is adamant, firmly entrenched in his position.

Chiefs Walker and Cavaglieri listen, try reason, try explaining their departments' gratuity policies, and even grovel a bit, all to no avail. Chief Cavaglieri even invoked his status as a long-standing member of the SFIAC, again all to no avail. Finally, the Chiefs looked at each other and shrugged.

"It looks like the nuclear option," Chief Walker said. Chief Cavaglieri concurs, and together they face Lorenzo, who is standing with his arms folded across his chest, defiant.

"Do you want to do the honors?" Chief Cavaglieri asked.

Walker agrees to start. "Lorenzo, we very much appreciate your generosity. However, your kindness, although well intended, and very much appreciated, puts both of us in a difficult position. We've tried talking, reasoning, and explaining, but you are insistent on not hearing us, and having it your way."

"That's correct. I'm the president of the club, and it will be my way."

"Lorenzo, you leave us no choice. Unless you accept payment from us for tonight's 'meeting,' we will be forced to do our jobs to their respective, fullest capabilities. There will be strict parking and double-parking enforcement, complete with citations, strict meter enforcement and tow away zones. Chief Cavaglieri's inspectors will be here daily to ensure there are no fire code or, heaven forbid, occupancy violations. In other words, we will make your life miserable."

Lorenzo invoking his best Chico Marx stated, "that's a no good."

Then he went on, "You wouldn't…"

"Oh, but we would. Let us pay, make us happy, and life goes on."

Chief Cavaglieri once again invoked his membership status and said something in Italian:

"*L'amicizia è tutto. L'amicizia è più del talento. È più del governo. È quasi uguale alla famiglia.*"

Lorenzo stood a little straighter. Then he unfolds his arms and throws up his hands in mock surrender. He starts to turn away, then turns back to face them.

"You may think you have won," he said, "but it's our club and you can't control the meal portions or the size of the drinks."

The two Chiefs look at one another, extend their hands to Lorenzo, and simultaneously say, "Deal."

As the Chiefs walk back into the main hall, Chief Walker can't stand it any longer.

"What did you say to Lorenzo?"

"Something from *The Godfather*," Chief Cavaglieri replied. "Friendship is everything. Friendship is more than talent. It is more than the government. It is almost the equal of family."

"It seemed longer than that," Chief Walker says, bunching his eyebrows together.

"Since I was on a *Godfather* roll," Cavaglieri points out, "I added that part of being able to make him a deal he couldn't refuse."

They both laughed.

Back in the main dining room, the 'meeting' is still in full swing. Everyone who worked on the case is exhausted and emotionally drained. The 'meeting' is a great stress reliever and an opportunity to thank all the members of the team.

Liam is particularly gregarious all evening. He personally thanked everybody, and even a number of people more than once. Which left him in no condition to drive. Kathy, anticipating this particular outcome, had made the necessary arrangements with John. While John would take Reggie home, Kathy struck some sort of bargain with Liam for her to be the designated driver, and she switched to club soda. As an additional part of the bargain, Kathy has reminded Liam that if he's too gregarious around a certain Profiler, his profile will be altered. Liam understands all too well. At just about 1:00 a.m., she and John assisted Inspector Donnelly into Kathy's car for the ride home.

The 'meeting' finally adjourned. San Francisco's finest Police and Fire personnel, accompanied by the stalwarts of the Federal Bureau of Investigation, start for the front of the building to a line of cabs, Uber and Lyft vehicles, and then home.

Back home in Noe Valley, Liam has managed to get into bed, with minimal assistance from Inspector Sullivan, and is about to slip away into slumber when he hears her say something about his part of the bargain. It is a bit foggy, but she certainly seems insistent that it be honored. He assures her that he would honor whatever the hell she is talking about... and he is out.

Kathy finishes locking up and putting things away, then climbs into bed, knowing tomorrow is going to be interesting.

CHAPTER 35

It is Monday morning. Lieutenant Lee has given all four principal Inspectors the day off. A good thing, because when Liam laboriously pulled himself up in bed, his eyes refused to comply. With a bit more cajoling and negotiating, they finally lift themselves, only to shut again when they encounter the bright light of morning. His head is throbbing, his stomach churning.

At least his nose and ears were working. And his mouth, unfortunately. The night before doesn't taste particularly good the morning after. But he smells coffee brewing, and hears Kathy moving around in the kitchen. He pulls on some clothes and stumbles into the bathroom, performing an abridged and perfunctory version of his morning ablutions, then drags his feet into the kitchen. When she hears his feet scuffing in, Kathy looks up at him and smiles.

231

"How can you be up and moving around at this ungodly hour on a Monday morning?" Liam asks. "And smiling, no less! I feel like shit."

"Well, that probably has something to do with the fact that I didn't try, singlehandedly, to add a second shift at the Jameson Distillery."

Liam smirks. "Aye, lass, just doin' me part to help the lads back home, in any way I can."

"I'm sure they probably have your framed picture enshrined in a hallowed position in their break room." Kathy opens a cabinet door and pulls out a mug. "Want some coffee?"

"It smells good," Liam concedes, "but to quote Willie Nelson, it's a Bloody Mary morning."

Kathy looks at him in disbelief. "Are you kidding me?"

"I am." Liam smiles. "You're a life saver, coffee sounds great. And after the resurrection is underway, I'll make us some breakfast."

"Sounds good." Kathy pours coffee into the mug and hands it to him. "Something light, though. Remember your part of the bargain? To drive to Napa today for a little wine tasting?"

"Ohhhh…" Liam says as he feels his stomach turn a little. "More liquor."

"This is perfect," Kathy says brightly, "Remember, I'll taste, and you are my designated driver."

"Deal. How about a couple of eggs and toast? Something simple."

"Sounds perfect. And while you're maxing out your culinary skills, I'll take a shower."

"You know, I'm going to give you a little piece of advice here: It's usually not very wise to insult the guy who's making your meal, especially when you're out of the room."

Kathy grins as she walks out of the kitchen, leaving Liam to his chores. He hears the shower come on and imagines the scene a couple of rooms away. Just for a moment, he considers getting undressed and joining her. But he remembers Napa and the bargain…sort of.

And breakfast isn't going to make itself.

"Smells wonderful," Kathy says as she breezes back into the kitchen. It always amazed Liam how quickly she could shower and get ready to go. That hasn't been his experience with other women in his past. But in the time it took him to fry some eggs and butter some toast, she is back and looking great.

"I hope you like it," Liam says as he places the plates on the table.

"I'm sure I will. Thanks."

"You're welcome."

They sat across from each other, eating their first few bites in silence. Liam, though initially turned off by the thought of breakfast, is experiencing a bit of rejuvenation.

"So," he says after another swallow of coffee, "where am I driving you in order that you may expand your viticultural horizons and I can fulfill my part of this bargain?"

"I was thinking we could start in St. Helena at Merryvale, then go to Hall, and maybe finish up at Bennet Lane in Calistoga."

"Uh huh," Liam nods. "And if I'm simply to be your chauffeur for the day, what's in it for me?"

"You mean besides the pleasure of my company?" Liam shrugs as if that were a given.

"Well, how about we have dinner at that little Mexican restaurant on Lincoln Street in Calistoga?"

"Oh, Pacifico?"

"That's the one," Kathy says, looking a little surprised. "How did you remember the name?"

"It's also the name of a very good Mexican beer."

Liam grins as he pushes the last bit of toast around his plate, sopping up the egg yolk.

"Ah, the alcohol connection," Kathy says, looking at him askance.

After chewing his last bite and washing it down with the last swallow of coffee, Liam returned her smile. "How about you throw the dishes in the dishwasher, and I'll grab a shower. Then, we can leave."

"You got a deal, mister."